It was the most overwhelming sensation going in there. I honestly think my heart stopped beating for a moment. I had a brief flash of every thought and feeling I'd ever had about Bob and Lorraine and David. The good times, the bad, all of it came over me. I could feel their presence there, not like ghosts, but just overwhelming memories. Bob drinking his Scotch and sodas. Lorraine cheerfully talking about the most intimate part of her life. And David ... So many images of David, pacing, lying down on the sofa, shoes deliberately kept on, sitting quietly in a corner, pretending not to be there. I walked into the living room and sat down, only because I had to sit down, or else I would have fainted.

SUSAN BETH PFEFFER is the author of *Starring Peter And Leigh* and *The Beauty Queen,* both available in Dell Laurel-Leaf editions. She has also written *Just Between Us, What Do You Do When Your Mouth Won't Open?,* and *Courage, Dana*—all available in Dell Yearling editions. She lives in Middletown, New York.

ABOUT DAVID

Susan Beth Pfeffer

LAUREL-LEAF BOOKS bring together under a single imprint out-standing works of fiction and nonfiction particularly suitable for young adult readers, both in and out of the classroom. Charles F. Reasoner, Professor Emeritus of Children's Literature and Reading, New York University, is consultant to this series.

Published by
Dell Publishing Co., Inc.
1 Dag Hammarskjold Plaza
New York, New York 10017

For Pat Allee,
who almost cried

ISBN: 0-440-90022-0

RL: 4.7

Reprinted by arrangement with Delacorte Press
Printed in the United States of America
First Laurel-Leaf printing—March 1982
Sixth Laurel-Leaf printing—April 1985

September 27

This is how I found out.

I was biking home from Steffi's, where I'd had supper. The sun had set, but I've biked at night long enough not to be frightened, even if Mom is. To get home from Steffi's, you pass David's house, and even though I was on my side of the street, it was impossible not to notice the police cars, with their rotating red lights, and the cops and the small crowd of people pressing at the barricades.

My heart started beating rapidly, and I pedaled as fast as I could to my house and down the driveway. I put the bike back in the garage, then ran to the back door. I searched through my pocketbook for my keys, but I couldn't find them, so I rang the bell.

"Go away. We're not talking to any reporters."

"Dad, it's me!" I shouted. I knew something awful had happened but I was too scared to try to imagine what.

"Are you alone?"

"Of course I am. Let me in."

Dad opened the door and grabbed my arm to pull me in. "Did anyone try to talk to you?" he asked.

"No." I said. "Daddy, what is it?"

He looked awful, pale and shaky. "I have something horrible to tell you," he said. "Maybe we'd better go into the living room and sit down."

"Where's Mom? Is Mom okay?" I asked. There was no logic to my question, but fear had won out, and I needed immediate reassurance.

"Your mother's fine," Dad said, as he led me into the living room. "Dr. Goldstein was here and gave her a sedative. She's resting now."

"And Jimmy?" I needed to know right away that my older brother was all right.

"He's fine too," Dad said. "I guess we'll have to call him, though, and tell him what happened."

"What did happen?" I asked, my nerves jangly from not knowing.

Dad motioned for me to sit on the sofa. I did, and he sat down next to me. He put his arm around my shoulder. Dad isn't usually a physically affectionate man, so I knew something monstrous must have happened.

"Tell me, Dad," I said, thinking God knows what. Robbery maybe. Kidnapping. One of those television crimes that have no reality in my world.

"It's David," Dad said. "And . . . his parents. They're dead, Lynn."

"David's parents are dead?" I asked. Bob and Lorraine dead? I couldn't picture it. Not Bob and Lorraine. They couldn't be dead. I'd known them too many years for them to die.

"Yes, honey," Dad said. "And David's dead too."

"Oh, my God," I said, I felt the blood rush out of my head. How could David be dead? He was only seventeen, my age. He was my oldest friend in the world, practically my brother. He couldn't possibly be dead. There had to be some kind of mistake. David and I would laugh about all this tomorrow. Where was David?

Dad held onto me more firmly. "Are you all right?" he asked. "The doctor left me something for you too, if you need it."

"No, Dad," I said, but I grabbed onto his hand as though he could keep me from drowning. "What happened?"

"We don't know yet," Dad said.

"Were they murdered?" I asked, thinking horrifying Charles Manson thoughts. It could have been my parents. It could have been me.

Dad held my hand, trying to give me his strength through touch. "No, honey. They don't think so."

"What do you mean?" I said. "Was it an accident?"

"I really don't know," Dad said. "But your mother was sort of a witness, and she didn't see anybody going into or coming out of the house."

"My God," I said again. "Mom saw it all?" Had she been forced to witness it all, a gun pressed to her head?

"No," Dad said firmly. "She did not."

I eased away from him slightly to let him know I wasn't about to faint. "What happened?" I asked. "From the beginning."

"I can only tell you what I know," he said. "All right. About an hour ago . . ."

"An hour ago?" I said. "They've only been dead an hour?" An hour ago. I'd been having dessert with Steffi, talking about our English assignment. And David was dying? Separate, alone, dying? How could

I not have known? How could I be eating a piece of apple pie while David died?

"About an hour ago," Dad began again. "Your mother was in the living room watching for you. She was perched on the window seat, not concerned, just kind of enjoying the night and the quiet. We'd already had supper, and I was in my den going over some papers. The windows were open, and she thought she heard two sharp, funny noises come from the Morrises' house. She might have ignored them except that almost immediately the lights went off there, and there was a third noise. Your mother couldn't be sure anything was the matter, so she called Lorraine, and there was no answer. She let the phone ring maybe twenty times, and then she came into the den to ask me what I thought." He paused for a moment, and looked down at his hands, before starting again. "I said I'd go over to check things out, but your mother had already decided something . . . well, she said we should call the police just in case. Worse came to worst, it would be a false alarm. So she called and told them what she'd heard and seen, and ten minutes later there was a squad car."

"Thank God, you didn't go over," I said. "Whoever did it might still be there."

"When I went over, about twenty minutes ago," Dad said, taking my hand again, "the reporters were there already, and a lot more policemen and doctors and photographers, but I spoke to some lieutenant. I told them I was the Morrises' lawyer, and I guess that and the fact that my wife made the phone call gave me the right to be told certain things. Honey, they're pretty sure it was a murder-suicide."

I broke away from him and ran out of the living room. I made it to the bathroom just in time, and threw up over and over again. I must have stayed in the bathroom for five minutes or more refusing to come out and face what Dad was telling me. David was just killed; had he killed as well? Had he really hated his parents that much? And himself? Was that hatred I'd always known that deep, that violent as well?

"Are you all right?" he asked, from the other side of the door.

"Yeah," I said, and ran more cold water on my face. "I'll be out in a minute."

"I wish I didn't have to tell you all this," he said.

"It's okay," I said, and came out. "I'm okay. Really. Dad, David didn't do it. Did he? He couldn't have."

"Of course they don't know for sure," Dad said. "They won't for a while, not until they've run certain tests. But there was a note."

"Somebody made him write the note," I said. "Dad, he couldn't have just done it."

"I don't know," he said. He looked ashen. Bob and Lorraine Morris had been close friends of his.

"Coffee," I said. "Would you like some coffee?"

"No, I'm okay," Dad said. "Let's sit down, okay? This has been a shock for all of us."

Instead we went into the kitchen. As we sat down, I noticed Mom's calendar. The twenty-ninth was circled in red. Two days away. Lorraine's birthday. She and Bob and Mom and Dad were supposed to have dinner together that night at the new French restaurant. Mom had been looking forward to it for weeks. I was planning to buy Lorraine something tomorrow. Mom had suggested a scarf. Lorraine liked scarfs.

"What did the note say?" I forced myself to ask. It was too easy to think about scarfs and birthdays and forget they weren't going to happen.

"I don't know," Dad said. "Just that there was one, and it was pinned to David's shirt."

"There must have been blood all over it," I said. "How could they read it if there was blood all over it? How could they know for sure it was his handwriting?"

"They don't know for sure it was his handwriting," Dad said. "They'll have to check it out with samples."

"Maybe it won't be," I said. "Maybe somebody made him write that note. Someone came in and murdered Bob and Lorraine and then made David write that note."

"Lynn, honey, I wouldn't get too convinced of that if I were you. The way David died . . . well, it's just not . . . it's more a way a suicide might do it than a murderer."

"How did he do it?" I asked.

Dad stared at me for a moment.

"Dad, he's dead," I said calmly. The calm was easy; I didn't believe a word I'd just said. "How did it happen?"

"He shot himself through his mouth," Dad said. "The bullet hit his brain. Death was instantaneous, and probably not painful."

"I don't believe you," I said. "Why didn't his parents stop him?"

"Honey, they were dead already."

"And David murdered them?" I asked. I'd lost all control over my voice. Everything came out in short horrible shrieks. "David shot his parents? Is that what you're saying? He murdered them?"

"That's what they think."

"Don't say they!" I screamed. "What do you think? Do you think David murdered his own parents?" Maybe if I screamed loud enough, I wouldn't have to think it.

Dad got up and walked over to the liquor cabinet. He took out the Scotch and poured two glasses, then handed me one. "Take this," he said. "It's medicinal." He downed the other himself.

I sipped it. The burning pain in my throat gave me something new to concentrate on, and after a shudder that seemed to take over my body, I felt better.

"Where's Mom?" I asked again.

"Sleeping," Dad said. "She was very shaken up. We all are."

"Did you . . . did you see . . . you know, the Morrises?"

"Yes," Dad said. "They asked me to make a positive identification."

"Oh, God," I said, and took another quick swallow. I started coughing.

"Are you all right?" Dad asked.

I swallowed hard a few times and nodded. "I'm okay," I said. "Really. I'm almost starting to believe it all."

"I know," Dad said. "It's almost easier to have seen the bodies. It convinces you of the impossible."

We heard footsteps and turned around. Mom was standing at the doorway.

"Hi," she said. "Is that Scotch? I could use some too."

"Should you?" Dad asked. "With the tranquilizer?"

"It's okay," she said. "I asked Dr. Goldstein before he left. He said it wouldn't kill me."

I got up and hugged Mom. "How are you?" I asked her. She looked pale, and her hands were cold and trembling.

"I'm awful," she said. "My head is still reeling. But I didn't want to be alone anymore. Can we stay in here? From the living room you can see the Morris house, and I don't want to."

"Of course," Dad said, and poured Mom a drink.

"Have you told Lynn everything?" Mom asked, as we all sat down again.

"I think so," Dad said. "Everything I know."

"He shot each of his parents once?" I asked.

"We think so," Dad said.

"And then he turned off the lights and shot himself," I said. It sounded so silly I wanted to laugh. People I know didn't kill.

"As far as we know," Dad said.

There was a knock on the front door. Dad walked to the living room. Mom and I sat in the kitchen and stared at each other. Neither of us knew what to say. We couldn't just make small talk. But I couldn't bear to ask Mom her version of what had happened.

"Damn reporters," Dad said when he came back. "I told them I had nothing to say and would continue to have nothing to say. And that they should leave my family alone. Not that they will. We're in for an awful evening."

That did it. I started laughing, and I couldn't stop for a very long time. Dad looked like he wanted to slap me, but he couldn't. I just waved him aside. I knew when I stopped laughing, the crying would begin, and I wasn't sure that once I started crying, I'd ever be able to stop.

September 28

None of us slept very well last night; we kept walking around and bumping into each other. Every time I'd almost fall asleep, I'd picture David, or Bob and Lorraine, at parties or talking or playing. Once I thought I heard David playing his guitar, but I was just dreaming. And I kept thinking about the lunch David and I had had that day. Just a normal everyday school lunch. But hard as I tried, I couldn't remember what we'd talked about. I'd almost grasp it, and then the memory would slip away.

This morning we decided to go about our usual business. So Dad went to the office, and Mom to the gallery, and I went to school. I tried not to think about walking to school alone, without David.

As I approached the school door, Steffi grabbed me by the arm and pulled me aside. Her eyes were red.

"Why didn't you tell me?" she asked.

"What?" I said, because I was startled by the question. I certainly knew what she was talking about.

"David. Why didn't you tell me?"

I thought back on the night before. "I was too upset," I said. "It didn't occur to me to."

"But you knew," she said.

"Yeah, I knew," I said.

"I had to find out on the radio today," she said. "That's how I woke up, with that on the news. Can you imagine how that felt?"

I couldn't imagine anything worse than biking past David's house and seeing the crowds and the police and everything else that happened last night, but I didn't say so. Instead I apologized, because I figured that was what Steffi wanted me to do.

"I loved David," she said. "You knew that."

I hated that past tense. I started walking away from Steffi and toward the school.

"I did!" Steffi shouted at me, and started to cry. "You know I did!"

The other kids started looking at her, and then at me. I just kept walking. Right then, I didn't have any comfort to hand over to Steffi.

Most of the other kids knew already also. A few of them came to me to ask if I knew anything more than they did, but I could honestly say I didn't. Except that Dad identified the bodies, and there was no reason to tell people that.

The teachers couldn't ignore what happened. We were all a bunch of zombies, except at an occasional odd moment when somebody would start crying. Mr. Glick, who likes the dramatic gesture, decided in English to provide a catharsis and read us a poem about early death. Steffi and Judd and a couple of other kids started crying, and Tommy got really mad and called Mr. Glick an unfeeling bastard. He got away with it too, I think, because Mr. Glick hadn't been expecting such a strong reaction.

Latin was the hardest, because there are only twelve of us in the class, and we felt David's absence the strongest. Mrs. Maguire tried at first to get us to concentrate on Virgil, but we all flubbed our translations, so she just put the book aside and let us talk. And we did. Not about David though; we all seemed to be avoiding talking about him, but about Mr. Glick and current events and Saturday's football game. Mrs. Maguire, who's the most no-nonsense teacher I've ever had, let us go on with our nonsense. And nobody cried.

In gym Miss Grey came over and told me to change back into my school clothes; I was wanted in the principal's office. So I went back to the locker room, changed, got my books, and walked to the office.

Mr. Steward, the assistant principal, met me at the door. "Come in, Lynn," he said. "Lieutenant Donovan would like to speak with you." For a moment I got disoriented and thought David had been arrested. But then I remembered he was dead. I couldn't figure out why the police were investigating.

I walked into Mr. Steward's office and saw a middle-aged man sitting there. He didn't look like a cop, not the kind I knew from street crossings, or the kind I've seen on TV going out on strike. He wasn't in uniform; maybe that was the difference.

"I'll leave you now," Mr. Steward said, and left, closing the door behind him. I felt sick to my stomach.

"Lynn," Lieutenant Donovan said. "Please sit down."

I did.

"Please relax," he said. "I'm investigating the Morris family deaths, and I'm asking questions of a few of David's friends."

"Should I have a lawyer here?" I asked. My voice squeaked.

Donovan smiled. "Your father's a lawyer, isn't he," he said. "Don't worry. I won't ask anything too personal. My interest is in David Morris, and why he did what he did."

"They know for sure that he did it?" I asked.

Donovan nodded. "He fired the gun," he said. "And we have no reason to assume he did it under duress. It seems to have been a voluntary act."

"What did his note say?" I asked.

"I'm sorry," he said. "We're not ready to divulge that information yet."

"I wouldn't tell anyone," I said, my voice rising. "I just wanted to know."

"I understand," he said. "And if I could tell you, I would. Now do you think you could tell me a few things about David?"

"I'll try," I said, on the alert against questions. I wasn't going to tell him everything, cop or no cop. I'd spent a lot of my life protecting David's secrets. It was a habit I couldn't just break, and certainly not to a stranger, a policeman. Not that I was sure which of David's secrets I should respect and which were meaningless now. It would take time to sort through all that.

"You knew David Morris for many years, didn't you?" Donovan began.

"Am I being taped?" I asked.

"No," he said. "Why?"

"You're not taking notes," I said.

"I'll write up my report after you leave," he said. "I find if I take notes, it distracts me from what the person is really saying."

"David and I were friends for a long time," I said.

"For how long?" he asked with a sigh.

"Since his parents bought the house across the street from mine," I said. "When he was four."

"Diagonally across," Donovan said.

"Diagonally across," I said.

"Your parents were friends too?" he asked.

"Yes," I said. If he wanted to know anything more about my parents, he could damn well ask them.

"Did David know he was adopted?" Donovan asked.

"Yes," I said, startled by the question. Donovan obviously meant to rattle me. I warned myself to stay on guard, to keep protecting David.

"When did he find out?" he asked.

"He always knew," I said. "His parents never made a secret of it."

"Was David at peace with himself about it?" Donovan asked.

I was silent for a moment. There was no point lying. "David wasn't at peace with himself about very much," I said.

"Including the adoption?"

"Including the adoption," I said. "Why? Did his note mention that?"

"Did he resent his natural parents for giving him up?" Donovan asked. "Or did he want to find them?"

I remembered the last time David and I talked about that. It was in August, at the end of the vacation. We'd been sitting on the front stairs of my house, staring at the stars and enjoying the breeze.

"It's killing me," he said that night. "I hate them, those anonymous people who created me, but I want to know them. I have to know them. Who were they? What led them to that moment? What led them to throw me out, like an extra puppy in a litter? How could they do that to me? How could they not care? And why should I care so much?"

"Lynn?" Donovan asked.

"He was ambivalent," I said, I knew it was stupid, but I just couldn't blurt out David's feelings.

"I'm not trying to hurt you," Donovan said. "And none of us can hurt David anymore."

"Then why are you asking me questions?" I asked. "David's dead, his parents are dead, what's to be gained?"

"Maybe, just maybe, if we know what motivates a David Morris, we'll be able to prevent some other kid from doing what he did," Donovan said.

"Do you really believe that?" I asked.

"Yes," he said. "Now, getting back to David. Would you say he was an angry boy?"

I nodded.

"His teachers have all presented me with quite a different view," Donovan said. "They say David was very well-mannered, very self-disciplined. They were sure he'd go to an Ivy League college and do quite well for himself. As a matter of fact, they were in a state of shock over what happened last night."

"You can be angry and still behave well," I said. "David compartmentalized his life. And his rage could be quite cold."

"What do you mean?"

"He was angry once at a friend of his," I said. It was a classic David story, one Donovan was sure to hear time and again that day. "And he didn't speak to him for two years. Not even to say hello or excuse me or please pass the salt. Just ignored him for two years."

"You mean he held a grudge?"

"No," I said, disliking Donovan more and more. "I mean David's rages burnt cold. Like dry ice."

"And was he in a state of rage with his parents? His adopted parents?"

When I was little I was fascinated by how much David hated his parents. I'd never seen anything like it. It was cold and it was continuous. Birthdays, holidays, special treats, nothing broke through that wall of hatred. Sometimes it heated up, and there would be fights, and he'd come to stay with us, or go to his friend Jeffrey. Sometimes it would be buried so deep that to look at him for the first time, you would never know he was anything but a loving, affectionate son. But it was always there. But I couldn't say any of that to Donovan.

"He must have been," I said instead. "He killed them, after all."

I got the strong feeling Donovan didn't like me any more than I liked him. I wondered if the other kids had been just barely cooperative. There was no warm feeling to the police where I lived, and it was possible he'd been met with resistance all day long. Resistance he was unlikely to understand. We were being loyal to someone he regarded as a murderer.

"Just a couple more questions," he said. "And then I'll let you get back to your classes."

"All right," I said.

"Did you regard yourself as David's best friend?"

"No," I said. "I was his oldest friend. Jeffrey Green

was his best friend." I wondered briefly how Jeffrey was. I'd hardly thought of him since last night. But of course I never liked Jeffrey.

"Oh, yes," Donovan said. "I wanted to talk with him, but he was absent."

"He's probably at home," I said. "I almost didn't come into school today."

"He and David were very close then?"

"Yes."

"Were they lovers?"

I stared at Donovan, my mouth wide open. "Go to hell," I said. Let him arrest me.

"I'm sorry," Donovan said. "But I have to ask these questions."

"No, you don't," I said. "David's dead. What does it matter?"

"It matters," he said. "Were they lovers?"

"Not to my knowledge," I said, trying to stay calm.

"And would you have known?"

"If I wouldn't have, why bother asking me?" I said. "May I be excused now?"

"Another minute," he said.

I crossed my arms and scowled.

"This isn't a game," Donovan said. "And believe me, I'm getting no pleasure out of it. I have kids myself. I wouldn't want anybody asking them the kinds of questions I've been asking you. But we have to know. What David did was a horrible sick act. And we have to know why."

"I don't know why," I said. I don't know. Not really. Not why David hated them so much then, that he did what he did. Just last night.

"Do you have any ideas?"

I shook my head. "David was unhappy," I said.

"But that was nothing new. I don't know what could have made him do it now, as opposed to years ago, or years from now."

"Were you surprised to learn that he had?"

"I was shocked," I said carefully. "I still am. Most of me doesn't believe any of this is happening."

"But were you surprised?" Donovan asked, looking straight at me.

"A little," I said. "Not as much as I should have been."

"When did you talk to him last?"

"Yesterday," I said. "At school."

"What did you talk about?"

"You're not going to believe this," I said, and realized I was blushing.

"Try me," he said.

"I don't remember," I said. "I honestly don't remember. I was up half of last night trying to remember."

"When did you talk?" he asked, cocking his head to one side.

"We had lunch together."

"And you can't remember any of it?"

I shook my head.

"It'll probably come back to you," Donovan said. "If it does, and it's important, will you call me?"

"Yeah," I said. "But it probably isn't anything. I probably forgot just because it was unimportant." I rubbed the top of the desk with my fingers.

"But it bothers you that you've forgotten."

"It bothers me a lot," I said. "Is that it?"

"Lynn, listen to me, all right?" Donovan said. "I want to know David, to understand him. I don't just want to hate him or feel revulsion or even just feel sorry for him. I want to understand what led him to the moment when killing was his only alternative. And I need your help. Because I think you loved him, as a friend, and I need to see David through the eyes of someone who loved him. So please, help me. I need your help."

I started crying then, and because I hate crying in public, I tried as hard as I could to stop the tears.

"Here," Donovan said, handing me a box of tissues.

Wordlessly, I took a tissue and blew my nose. I gulped down the rest of my tears. There was something else I had to say to Donovan. Something nobody else might know to tell him.

"Please," I said, trying to sound rational. "There's something you have to understand."

"All right," Donovan said gently.

"Bob and Lorraine," I said, and my body shuddered convulsively. I took a deep breath, held it, and exhaled slowly. "They were my parents' friends, and I'm not saying they deserved to die. What David did was . . . But they were very hard on him. He didn't hate them without cause."

"No," Donovan said. "I expect he didn't."

"They abused him," I said. "More than most parents do, I think. And they made demands on him, constant demands, he couldn't possibly hope to achieve. If he got a 90, they expected a 95. If he got a 95, they expected a 100. And if he got a 100 they wanted to know why he didn't get them more often."

Donovan nodded.

"He worked," I said. "He worked for every grade he got. He spent more time on homework than anybody I know. He studied for his SAT's months before the exams. He did extra assignments. He never spoke back to his teachers because he was terrified they'd take it out in his grades. He'd argue for hours with teachers over a single point on an essay exam."

"Maybe it was important to him," Donovan said.

"It wasn't." I said. "He couldn't have cared less. David loved science fiction and photography and playing the guitar. But his parents wanted him to be valedictorian. Nothing less would satisfy them. He couldn't even keep the guitar at his house. He played it at my house, so his parents wouldn't know he was wasting time on it. And they hated it when he read science fiction. They said he was rotting his mind. Anything that wasn't about school rotted his mind."

"Is that why he hated his parents?"

"Wouldn't you?" I asked. "They never praised him. Never. I never once heard them say anything nice to him. And I knew him for thirteen years. Not once."

"What did your parents think?"

"Parents side with parents," I said. "But they let David stay at our place anytime he wanted. And they let him keep his guitar there. And I know they worried about him."

"Thank you, Lynn," Donovan said, getting up. "I know how hard this has been for you. Do you want to go back to your classes now?"

"No," I said. "I'm going home. I have to be alone for a while. Would you please tell Mr. Steward that I'm taking the rest of the day off? And if he doesn't like it, tell him to lump it."

Donovan grinned. "I'll tell him," he said. "But not in quite those words."

I managed a small smile back, got up, grabbed my books, and ran all the way back home.

I could hear the phone ringing when I got in. I

was tempted not to answer it, for fear it was a reporter or a cop, but after the tenth ring, I picked it up. The ringing hurt my stomach.

"Hello?" I said.

"Lynn? It's Jimmy."

"Jimmy!" I cried.

"What's going on there?" he asked.

"Oh, Jimmy," I said. "David and his parents . . ."

"I know," he said. "It was in the paper. I just saw it. Lynn, what's going on? Are Mom and Dad okay? The article said Dad found the . . . found them."

"He did," I said. "Mom heard the shots, and Dad went over. They're okay, I guess. I guess we all are."

"The papers weren't wrong then," he said. "David really did . . ."

"Yeah," I said, wanting to cry again.

"God," Jimmy said. "I kept hoping the papers made it up. I know that's crazy, but I couldn't help hoping."

"I know," I said.

"Do you think I should come home?" Jimmy asked. "What are they doing about a funeral?"

"I don't know," I said. "I don't even know who would be making the arrangements."

"I could be home late tonight," Jimmy said.

"No," I said, although I wanted him to come home more than anything. "It would really bother Mom and Dad if you missed school because of all this. I'll tell them you called, and maybe they'll call you tonight."

"Oh, Jimmy," I said. "I'm just starting to hurt. And it hurts so much."

"I know," he said. "I loved David too."

"I'm going to start crying," I said.

"Go cry," he said. "I'll talk to you all tonight."

"Okay," I said. "Thanks for calling, Jimmy."

"God," he said. "I mean you're welcome. Take care, Lynn."

I hung up the phone and wished I had told Jimmy to come straight home. I always needed Jimmy when things were really bad. That's the function of big brothers in my opinion, to help their little sisters when their worlds are collapsing. And Jimmy does that better than most big brothers. Maybe he'll come home anyway, in spite of what I told him. It would be so great to have him here tomorrow to help me understand and grieve. Dante had a tour guide through hell; I don't see why I can't have one too.

September 29

Lorraine's birthday. Maybe because of that, maybe because it just took us all a couple of days to comprehend, we all took the day off. Dad, who never skips work, was the one to announce we should all stay in for the day. So we did. At various points we separated, I think mostly to cry in private, but for the most part, we stayed in the same room together. Dad's den usually, because it faces the backyard. The leaves are

changing and the view is beautiful. I went to my bedroom for a while and tried to study, then went back
to the den to announce I was going to bed.

"Lynn," Mom said. "Could you wait a minute?"

"Sure, Mom," I said. "What is it?"

She looked awful. When I noticed Dad, he looked
just as bad. They both looked so much older than
they did just a few days ago.

"Lynn, honey," Mom began. "Please, don't misin-
terpret this. But there's something we have to know."

I felt the way I had when Donovan had been
asking the questions. I would have made the same re-
quest for a lawyer, but my stomach hurt too much for
jokes.

"Lynn, did David ever say anything to you . . ."
Dad said. "What we want to know is if you had any
idea . . ."

"Oh, God," I said.

"I know he didn't say anything like 'Lynn, I'm going to . . .'" I could see Dad was struggling with
the words. "But did you have any idea? Did he give
you any idea what he was planning?"

"We don't know he planned anything," I said.
"Maybe he just did it."

"I don't think that's very likely," Dad said. "David
always thought about what he was going to do."

I don't know why I want to think David hadn't
planned all this in advance, but it's important to me.
"David didn't say anything to me," I said. "Absolutely nothing. Are you satisfied?"

Mom and Dad looked like they were. If I could
only remember what it was David and I talked about
at lunch, I might be satisfied too.

September 30

Tracy Sanders knows everything. I think it's because everybody confides in her. She has an earth mother look to her, and I've never seen her do anything cruel. Even David liked her, and David didn't really like many of the kids in our class.

She came up to me before classes began and said, "I think there's some thing you ought to know. Just so it won't throw you."

"What is it?" I asked, my stomach returning to its now familiar state of churning.

"There's a rumor going around about you."

"Great," I said. "What?"

"It's a theme with variations," she said. "One version goes that you're pregnant with David's child. Another that you were pregnant, but had an abortion."

"You're kidding," I said.

"I wish I were," she said. "It isn't just you, of course. The rumors have been flying around here about everybody. But I thought you ought to know."

"Jeffrey too?" I asked.

"Of course," she said. "He and David were planning to run off to Mexico together when David's parents found them. Stuff like that."

"It's Donovan's fault," I said. "He asked me about Jeffrey, and I'll lay odds he asked other kids about me. That's all it takes. One well-placed question."

"I don't think there's anything you can do," she said. "Except hold your head up high."

"Stiff upper lip and all that," I said. "Or maybe just shove my belly out and really give them something to talk about."

Tracy giggled nervously.

"Don't worry," I said. "And thanks for the warning. At least when I hear the whispers I'll know what they're about. That's a help."

"How's it going?" she asked.

"It's awful," I said. "My mother, well, she keeps crying, and I'm not much better. My father's shaky too, but he has a macho thing about crying in front of me."

"I just can't believe it," she said. "David doing something like that. Can you?"

"Oh, yeah," I said. "The more time passes, the more I can believe the whole damn thing."

October 2

A weekend, blessedly a weekend. Time off. Lots of phone calls, but except for that, peace and quiet. Mom's crying less, and so am I. Except for the dreams I've started to have, things seem better.

October 5

The dreams persist.

Some of them are classic nightmares. I hear gunshots, I see Lorraine, the terror on her face. I see Bob, already dead, a hideous grin on his face. Or David is chasing after me, brandishing a gun,

shouting at me not to worry, he just wants to show
me something.

Those I can handle. I wake up shaking, go to the
kitchen, mostly to get out of the bedroom, and make
myself some warm milk. Mom's standard cure for bad
dreams. Then, when I'm no longer scared, I go back
to my bedroom and after a little while, I fall back
asleep.

The worst nightmares are the ones that seem so
real. David and I are talking, about school or the
latest book he's read or maybe we're just gossiping.
Lorraine comes into the house, looking happier than
I've seen her in years. Sometimes it's Bob. He kisses
me on the forehead, says I'm getting prettier and
prettier.

Or we're younger somehow, and Jimmy is teasing
us, the way he did when we tried to tag after him.
Then he softens and agrees to play with us after all,
and the three of us sit under the oak tree and tell
riddles.

When I wake up from those dreams, I feel peaceful
at first, because the dreams are so peaceful. Then I
remember the truth. It's never easy to remember; it
always takes a few seconds. And it's like being told all
over again. I feel it always in my stomach, a sharp in-
take of air, and then I feel lightheaded and disbeliev-
ing.

Last night I dreamt that David and I were having
lunch together, the way we had the day he died, the
way we'd had a thousand times before. Only this time
he's telling me something and I can't hear him. The
noise in the cafeteria is so loud that even though he
is shouting, I can't make out a word he's saying. I
shout back for him to scream if necessary; I know it's

important for me to understand what he needs to tell me, but it doesn't help. He can't hear me either. And we sit there, trying to read each other's lips, drowning in noise and frustration.

Needless to say, I'm not sleeping very well these days.

October 6

For the past week, I've been avoiding eating in the cafeteria.

At first I thought it was just a natural distaste for the food they serve, but today I threw a real tantrum when Steffi insisted we eat there. The way she looked at me really worried me.

The high school cafeteria is a hell of a place to have a phobia about. But I realized it's that dream I had about David. Not being able to hear.

Anyway, when I started crying, Steffi gathered me together and took me to the girls' room where she calmed me down, told me I should see my doctor, and agreed to go to Juniors for lunch instead. She also said that she was very worried about Jeffrey, which is certainly understandable. He's missed more school than he's been in, and when he does come to class, he sits absolutely still, and sometimes he just starts shaking. I know what those shakes are like, but it's really awful seeing someone else going through them. I keep meaning to talk to him, but I've never liked him or enjoyed talking with him, and I've been avoiding him. I just know it wouldn't make either of us feel better if we shared our grief.

Jeffrey's never been my idea of an emotionally stable person, which I think is why David liked him so much. There weren't many people David felt less neurotic than. It bothered me a lot that Steffi mentioned him at the same time that she told me I should see my doctor.

I wonder what she would say if she knew my latest habit. Twice this week, at 2:00 a.m. or later, I called Jimmy at New Hampshire. I woke up half his dorm to do it.

The first time I scared him, and I spent most of five minutes reassuring him that everybody was fine; I just needed to hear his voice. The second time he was more annoyed than anything else until I started to cry. Then he offered to come home, and of course I told him not to. But I wanted him to come home more than anything. I always feel safer when Jimmy's around.

Mom told me yesterday that there wouldn't be a funeral for the Morrises. Bob's brother apparently took it upon himself to make the arrangements, and he had all the bodies cremated. He then took the ashes and scattered them, Bob's and Lorraine's together, David's all alone. He said there might be a memorial service later on, but he wasn't sure. I guess there's no way there could be a service for David. But I wish there could be. I still picture him as two people, and one is my friend.

There's also apparently quite a mess about the estate, since Bob left it all to Lorraine, and Lorraine left all her stuff to Bob and David. David didn't make out a will, so I'm keeping his guitar. It sits in my closet, and whenever I look at it, I think of David. Keeping it is not the smartest thing I've ever done, but I'm hoping there'll come a day when I can look at it and just feel vague warm feelings about David.

I doubt it though. Whenever I do think of him, which is almost constantly, my thoughts are mostly grief and horror. I loved David, the way you love a friend you've had since before kindergarten, and I thought I knew him. Yet he killed his parents. How could he have done it, pulled the trigger, not once but twice, three times, if you count his own final death. And why did he turn the lights out? David was always terrified of the dark; the last I'd heard, from Bob of course, he still slept with a night-light.

And if we were such good friends, why didn't he come to me? My parents, whom he was very close to, might have been too adult for him to confide in, and Jimmy, who he always looked up to, was too far away, but I was right there, ready to listen. I always had in the past; I would have then. And I could have told him to go into therapy, to talk out his feelings of rage and desperation with a professional.

Talk to your doctor. Just like Steffi told me.

Of course maybe he did say something like that to me, and maybe I did make the same hollow suggestion to him that Steffi made to me. I still can't remember just what we said that last day. Except I know I'm bothered by it. But that could just be the itching failure to remember.

The bad dreams continue.

October 12

So there I was, standing in front of the cafeteria, with Steffi insisting that I go in, when Jeffrey ran out, grabbed me by the shoulder, and said, "I've got to talk to you."

Steffi gave both of us a dirty look, but didn't say anything as Jeffrey led me outside. I know at some point I have to go in there, but I think it can wait a few days more. I keep seeing David in there, but I can't hear what he's saying.

Anyway, Jeffrey led me to a quiet section of the grounds, and we sat down even though it was pretty cool for this time of year. But he had a look in his eyes that I wasn't about to argue with.

"They're talking about us," he said.

"What?"

"You and me and David," he said. "They're saying we were all lovers."

It was all I could do not to laugh. Jeffrey is short and fat and has terrible acne. His father's a dermatologist, which makes it even funnier. I was about as likely to make love to him as to a mole.

"Who's saying it?" I asked, as gently as I could. After all, there had been constant swirls of rumors, especially right after David died, and I had featured in some, as had Jeffrey.

"Everybody," he said. "They're all talking about us. Can't you tell?"

"Calm down, Jeffrey," I said. "I haven't heard anything like that. Where did you hear it?"

"I heard Mr. Glick tell Mrs. Maguire," Jeffrey said, looking around to make sure no one was listening. "Even the teachers are tallking about it."

I could certainly see Mr. Glick in the role of a gossip. Mrs. Maguire was harder to picture. "What exactly did you hear?" I asked.

"Mr. Glick said 'they were all in it together,' " Jeffrey said. "That's a direct quote. 'They were all in it together.' "

"He might not have been talking about us," I said, putting my arm around Jeffrey.

"Don't touch me," he said, breaking away from me. "Do you want to give them more to talk about?"

"All right," I said, and edged away from him. Even for Jeffrey, this was not normal behavior.

"They were talking about us," Jeffrey said. "It was obvious. They think we were all lovers, and we killed David's parents together and then you and I shot David. That's what everybody thinks."

"Nobody thinks that," I said, as calmly as I could. "Don't you think if anybody really thought that, the police would have questioned us as suspects?"

"They questioned me," he said.

"Yeah?" I said. "When?"

"Right after David died," Jeffrey said. "Some guy named Donovan. He even asked if you and David were lovers."

"Oh, that," I said, and smiled in relief. "Look, Jeffrey, he asked me the same question about you and David."

It was the wrong thing to say. Jeffrey jumped up, and looked ready to fly.

"Wait a second," I said. "Calm down, Jeffrey. Donovan didn't know anything. He was just asking all the rude questions he could think of."

"They're going to arrest me," Jeffrey said.

"No, they aren't," I said, in my best no-nonsense voice. "Look, where were you when David's parents died?"

"I was home," Jeffrey said. "I was having supper with my family. I swear it."

"I believe you," I said. "I was at Steffi's. They can't possibly think we did it if we have such good alibis."

"Alibis can be broken," he said, but he was calmer.

"Not if they're true," I said. "It's okay, Jeffrey. Really. And even if people are gossiping about us, that'll stop."

He sat down next to me, and once again he was just old dumpy Jeffrey. "I should have known somehow and been able to talk him out of it."

"We couldn't," I said. "David didn't even hint he was going to do anything like that."

"Maybe not to you," Jeffrey said.

I felt a wave of irrational jealousy. David had spent more time with Jeffrey than he had with me, but I refused to believe he would confide something that important to a twirp like Jeffrey when I was right across the street. And then I felt guilty for having such awful thoughts.

"Did David tell you anything?" I asked.

But I'd lost Jeffrey again. "I'm not telling you," he said. "You'd just tell the police."

"All right," I said, and got up. "Let me know if you want to talk again, Jeffrey."

"Never," he said. "They'll find us out if we do."

"Yeah," I said, leaving Jeffrey to his paranoid fantasies. Of course I didn't go to the cafeteria. Instead, I ran over to the little luncheonette and grabbed a quick sandwich. It didn't matter. I didn't have much appetite right then. Mostly I wished I could be sure that what I told Jeffrey was the truth. That we couldn't have stopped David. That I couldn't have.

October 13

A doozy of a dream

I'm talking with David, and he tells me he has a secret just for me. I feel vaguely flattered I've been chosen for this secret, and I beg him to tell me right away.

David says he'll tell me, and we go to the school cafeteria (where else?), where he whispers so softly I can't possibly understand what he's saying. I beg him to tell me, and he says he will if I stand right in front of him. I move over there. I have to know, and I see he's pointing a gun right at me.

I called Jimmy right after I woke up.

October 14

The *New York Times* sent a reporter to the school today to talk to David's friends. I can't understand this late burst of curiosity, except that in White Plains last night a similar incident occurred. A boy there, also from a well-to-do family, killed his father, two sisters, and himself. His mother is on the critical list.

It's really awful. Everybody is so shaky around here anyway; we didn't need another incident like that.

I refused to talk to the reporter, since I didn't see how it could possibly do David or his family any good to have the *Times* dragging it all up again. But a lot of kids did talk to her. I guess it was the idea of being interviewed by the *Times*. The rotten bastards.

October 17

I'm still shaking, and I'm not sure I'll ever stop. This just isn't fair. None of it. I'm so frightened, and angry too. This must be how David felt most of the time, this awful combination of fear and hate.

First of all, it wasn't the world's greatest weekend. Saturday Mom got the phone bill and discovered I'd made five phone calls to Jimmy (there are another two or three that'll show up on the next bill). Jimmy, who's always been very protective of me, never told her or Dad about my midnight phone calls, and I guess at this point his dorm is used to them.

It wasn't that Mom and Dad were mad exactly. Concerned and perplexed would be more accurate. Why hadn't I told them I was calling Jimmy? Why was I bothering him so late at night? Couldn't I tell them what the matter was? Didn't I know they loved me?

These are the kind of questions there are no answers to. I explained that I woke up a lot of times late at night, after bad dreams, and I simply needed to turn to Jimmy. I've always turned to him in really bad times; they must know that. He was the one that used to scare my boogeymen away, never Mom or Dad. And Jimmy had been very loving and supportive when I called him, so I kept doing it. The nights I tried not to call, I couldn't fall back asleep.

I was instructed that if I could not bring myself to wake them up in the middle of the night, after a bad dream, I should write Jimmy a letter. Right then and there. Get out of bed, turn on the light, and write him a letter. At my desk. Just put down what I'd be telling him on the phone.

"The poor boy has to sleep too," Mom said.

I agreed to this perfectly nonsensical plan, and I'll try to stick with it. I've been feeling bad about waking Jimmy up all the time, which of course never stopped me.

So Saturday night, after my now almost nightly awful dream, I got up and wrote Jimmy exactly what I'd dreamed about. Not that I'd ever mail the letter (the dream involved horrible sexual permutations of Jeffrey, David, and me). And then I went back to bed and didn't fall asleep for close to three hours.

Sunday I was silent and grouchy.

Monday, today, I woke up tired, although I did sleep all the night through for the first time in ages. When I went downstairs to breakfast, Mom and Dad had that "how-are-we-going-to-cope-with-this-one" look on their faces.

"What is it?" I asked. I didn't see how things could possibly get worse.

"You might as well show her," Mom said to Dad. "She'll see it at school anyway."

So Dad handed me the *Times*. And there, right smack on the front page, was a picture of David and his parents. I even remembered when the picture had been taken.

The article really wasn't all that bad. A lot of it was about David, but more was about the kid in White Plains (his mother died yesterday). It was about the pressure to do well in school, the need for good grades to get into Ivy League colleges, and how some kids just can't take it. David's adoption was touched on, but not in any great detail. The article didn't mention me by name, but it did mention Jeffrey and Steffi and a couple of others.

What the article did have was David's suicide note. I guess by this time the police were ready to release it; it was no longer newsworthy, and that's why I hadn't seen it anywhere else. With all that's been going on, I'd practically forgotten about it.

David wrote: "Forgive me, but this is the only way to prevent further tragedy. I take full responsibility for the deaths of both my parents and myself."

I wish I knew what he meant by further tragedy. It hadn't occurred to me before that David thought worse things were going to happen. What was he afraid of? It must have been something enormous if he couldn't talk to me about it. And as far as I know, he didn't talk to Jeffrey. I wonder if I'll ever find out what it was, what could have been so dreadful to make him do what he did.

School, naturally, was buzzing. About half the conversations centered on just what David had meant by his suicide note. The other half were raging arguments over whether the kids who spoke to the reporters should have. I didn't think they should have, and I participated in those debates. I just didn't have the heart to speculate in public about what David meant.

For Christ's sake, he killed his parents, wrote the
note, pinned it on his shirt, turned the lights out, and
put the gun in his mouth. He was alone then more
than he'd ever been before, more than any of us
could ever imagine. It seemed dirty to stand around
wondering out loud just what he meant by those
words, like it was a difficult song lyric.

I didn't realize just how much I resented the kids
who spoke to the reporter until Steffi came up to me,
and I turned away from her. Steffi and I have been
best friends since eighth grade, and we've had our
share of spats, but this was different. This was that
cold hostile feeling. She was hurt by my reaction, so I
told her as best I could that it was possible later on
I'd feel better about it, but right then she'd better
leave me alone.

She accepted it, although she wasn't happy. Neither was I, so I didn't waste too much sympathy on
her. She could have refused to talk to the goddamn
reporter, the way a lot of the kids did.

Anyway, everybody's nerves were on edge even be-
for school began. But I kept thinking that when
classes began things would get better. We'd be dis-
tracted and the talking would stop.

I'm not exactly sure how it did happen. I know we
were in Glick's class—all of us—Jeffrey, Steffi, Judd,
and the rest of us. David's seat remains empty, and
we can't help looking at it, since he sat in the exact
middle of the room.

Glick's an idiot, but I almost don't blame him for
what happened today. He decided to grab the bull by
the tail, and since we were bound to have David on
our minds, he decided to skip the regular day's assignment and tell us about Thomas Chatterton.

Chatterton, whom I'd never heard of before, was a British poet who killed himself when he was seventeen and was starving to death anyway. Under other circumstances, it might have been interesting. Glick knows a lot of obscure stuff, and he likes to dramatize. But we were all so keyed up, he would have done much better to discuss Tennyson or Longfellow or one of those other guys who lived to be a hundred.

Things weren't too bad in the beginning. But then Glick got to the part about his suicide (rat poison, I think), and Jeffrey suddenly started screaming.

At first I couldn't understand what he was shouting, but then I realized he was saying, "NO! NO! I DIDN'T DO IT! I SWEAR!" Over and over again. Just blood-curdling screams.

At which point, a half-dozen kids started crying. Jeffrey's screams just set them off. Instead of sending one of us to get the nurse, Glick panicked and ran out of the room. And Tracy, who could calm a hysterical bull elephant, went over to Jeffrey. She tried to stroke his arm, but he jumped away from her, the way he had from me, and he started calling her a murderer.

Tracy didn't give up. She kept talking to Jeffrey in the calmest voice I've ever heard, and for one moment I thought she'd succeeded, since Jeffrey grew silent. But then he screamed again, just a wordless shriek.

Mr. Rice, who teaches in the room next to ours, came in when Jeffrey shrieked, and when he saw Glick wasn't there, he stayed with us, not that there was anything he could do. Jeffrey had run into a corner, and stood there screaming. Tracy followed him to the corner, and Judd tried to join her, but when Jeffrey saw him he started swinging his arms. He hit Tracy in the jaw and knocked her down. She started crying then.

We watched all of this. I felt vaguely like I should go over to Tracy, or maybe talk to Jeffrey, but I couldn't move. It was like my body wouldn't do anything except sit frozen on the seat. Finally Judd went over to Tracy, picked her up, and took her back to her desk.

So then Mr. Rice went over to Jeffrey, who shouted something about killing him. Mr. Rice stood about three feet away and tried to calm Jeffrey down by asking innocuous questions: What's your name? How old are you? And Jeffrey calmed down. He just started whimpering, which sounded awful, but was so much better than those screams. I felt such relief. This was all going to end with things back to normal.

Mr. Rice said to Jeffrey that he ought to go to his seat, and he took Jeffrey's hand and led him back to the desks. Only he went past Jeffrey's desk and took him to David's, which was much more conspicuously empty.

Jeffrey almost sat down in the chair. His legs brushed against it, and it was like the desk was on fire. He jumped away, knocking all the books on Steffi's desk onto the floor, which got her crying, and he ran to the front of the classroom, grabbed an eraser, and held it like a weapon.

Mr. Rice tried to get close to him again, and Jeffrey shook the eraser at him shouting something about murder. The eraser was full of chalk dust, and Mr. Rice got a lungful of it and started coughing uncontrollably.

That set four kids off. They began laughing, and they couldn't stop any more than the criers. Or Jeffrey.

At that point, Mrs. Maguire came in. She took one look at us, and then said in her sharpest voice, "Stop it! All of you. I said stop it!"

And we did. Mr. Rice stopped coughing, and the laughers stopped laughing, the criers started sniffling instead. And Jeffrey stopped screaming.

We stayed like that, like frozen statues, until Mr. Glick came back with the nurse. Mrs. Maguire took Mr. Glick into the hallway and gave him hell, Mr. Rice dusted himself off, which produced one final set of titters, and went back to his classroom. The nurse walked over to Jeffrey and asked him if he could accompany her back to her office. At first Jeffrey resisted, but when Mrs. Maguire came back into the room, he went with them.

The buzzer rang then, for the end of class, but none of us could move. We just sat there until way past the second buzzer. The class that usually comes in after us stood in the hallway until we could get up and leave. I guess we were all about five minutes late to our next class, but none of the teachers asked us about it. It doesn't take long for a story like that to get around school.

In Latin Mrs. Maguire said that Jeffrey had been taken to see a doctor, and she was going to entertain no nonsense that day. So we translated Virgil. Shakily maybe, but we did translate.

I must have been asked a hundred questions that day from kids who aren't in my English class, but I couldn't answer them. I couldn't even really remember what happened until I sat down and put it on pa-

per just now. It all was madness in the room then, all
that screaming and crying and laughing. And the
look on Tracy's face when Jeffrey hit her.

Dear God, don't let me turn into Jeffrey.

October 19

Jeffrey was taken to a hospital Monday night.
Rumors, which have been rampant for weeks now,
reached new heights. The truth, as far as I can figure
out, is that he's currently under observation. He's had
a severe breakdown (there are at least thirty witnesses
to that fact), and nobody's too optimistic that he'll
finish out the school year here.

Tracy, who's sporting a bruise on her jaw but no ill
feelings toward Jeffrey, asked me something funny today.

"Do you believe in curses?" she asked.

"What do you mean?" I said.

"It just seems to me like this whole class is under a
curse," she said. "Not like voodoo or anything magi-
cal, but just doomed. Do you know what I mean?"

The awful thing is I did know. We were always
told we were the best class that's come along in a long
time. Our grades were higher, our manners were bet-

ter. We had national prize winners in our class. Teachers liked us. We did well. We were achievers. We were studious and all of us were going to go to college. Even the class rebels were creative and won prizes. We seemed charmed.

But now there's David and Jeffrey. And last spring Judd was driving home on a date with Annie Pollack when his car was sideswiped by a drunk driver and he lost control and skidded into a tree. Judd broke both his legs, and Annie's still in the hospital after three back operations. They're not sure she's going to be able to walk again.

I've never been close to Judd, and I don't know him all that well, but it didn't surprise me when he was crying that awful first day after David died. He still won't drive.

And now that I think about it, that wasn't the first thing. Last fall they found out that Charlie Moskowitz had Hodgkin's disease. He's in remission now, and for all they know he's going to bury all of us. But it was the first touch of mortality any of us had had.

Things like that must happen in a lot of schools. Cancer, car accidents, suicide, breakdowns. It's just that it seems to have fallen on us all at once, and we were so unprepared. It's left all of us so shaky.

Yesterday Mr. O'Shea gave us a surprise history quiz. Today he apologized and said he'd torn the papers up. He'd planned the surprise quiz weeks ago, he said, but he should have realized when the day actually came that none of us were capable of handling a surprise anything just then.

October 21

Steffi called me up last night and asked me if I thought the article in the *Times* (the second one, with the note) had contributed to Jeffrey's breakdown.

I said yes. Jeffrey had seemed on the verge of one since David died, but I didn't think it was a coincidence he went crazy the day the *Times* article appeared. Steffi sounded awful. She said she was sorry, she hadn't meant to cause such awful trouble.

I said she shouldn't be apologizing to me. Jeffrey was the one who'd have to forgive her.

So she hung up. It took me a moment to realize what an awful thing I'd said, and once I did, I called her back. When somebody comes to you with irrational guilt, you're not supposed to tell her it's rational.

Steffi's mother answered the phone and when I asked for Steffi, she said Steffi was much too upset to come to the phone. I hung up even before I said who I was, although I'm sure Mrs. Zimmer knew.

Steffi didn't call me back last night, which didn't help me sleep. I'd think about Steffi and that would make me realize how much I missed David. He always took my side when Steffi and I fought. I'd lost him as an ally. And that made me hurt even more. I resolved that I would speak to Steffi first thing at school today. But the way things worked out, I didn't have a chance to talk to her alone until right before lunch. She started walking toward the cafeteria and I followed her.

"I'm sorry," I said, as soon as I had the chance. "That was a rotten thing I said to you last night, and I've been miserable about it ever since."

Steffi looked at me. "Are you ever going to forgive me about talking to the reporter?" she asked.

I'd been expecting a quick reconciliation (it hurt like hell being mad at Steffi for this long) and was taken aback by the question. "I don't think so," I said, which actually softened the truth a bit. Not that she appreciated it.

"What do you know?" she said scornfully. "You don't even have the nerve to go into the cafeteria. Just because of David and that last day."

Cheap shot. Accurate maybe, but cheap.

"That's not true!" I said. "Watch!" And I plowed my way through a line of kids and walked right into the cafeteria.

Steffi ran in after me, and when she saw me standing there (just barely too; my knees were like jelly), she hugged me. We hugged and laughed and didn't care what anybody thought. So then we went back on line, got our trays of food, and sat down at our customary table (how many meals had I eaten there with David?) and ate.

Of course Steffi spent the entire meal studying me for clinical signs, and I in turn tried hard not to supply them. Judd joined us and Tracy and Paul, and being with people helped. It wasn't as though I expected David's ghost to grab me and take me to whatever hell it's currently residing in, and I wasn't expecting to throw a screaming fit either, the way Jeffrey did, but my stomach lurched and I knocked over the salt and dropped my bread and was slightly short of breath the entire time I was there.

I hope now that I've proved I can do it, people won't expect me to keep eating there. I think I'm allergic to it.

October 23

I suppose I should have known we were going to have this conversation sooner or later, but it still startled me when Mom said she and Dad wanted to talk to me about something important. I followed her into Dad's den.

"First of all," Dad said, "I hope you realize that your mother and I love you very much."

"We've been very worried about you," Mom said. "The way you've been since David died."

I made a quick inventory of just how I'd been since then. Nightmares, insomnia, midnight phone calls, cafeteria phobia, occasional inexplicable shaking fits, loss of appetite followed by uncontrollable eating jags. Apathy toward school work. No desire for any sort of social life. Of course Mom and Dad didn't know about all those things, but even if they knew about half, I could understand their concern.

"Things have been rough," I said, in the understatement of the year. "I think they're going to improve though."

"Honey, we care about you," Mom said. "What you've been through this past month would hurt anybody. I'm not the same as I was a month ago, and neither is your father. But you've had to do a lot of growing up in a very short time, and we haven't been able to help as much as we'd like."

"It's okay," I said. "You've been there. I've known that."

"It is not enough," Dad said. "Your mother and I have talked about this a lot, and we think it would be a good idea if you saw a psychologist."

"You think I'm going to end up like Jeffrey?" I said.

"No, of course not," Dad said.

"What if I don't want to go?" I asked.

"We won't make you," Mom said. "And we won't pressure you, because that's the last thing you need right now. But we hope you'll give the idea serious thought and not just reject it."

I remembered another symptom. When I bike home now, if I'm going the direction that takes me past David's house, I go around an extra block so I won't have to. I can walk past the house (although I prefer not to), and since my bedroom windows look out at the house, I'm used to seeing it and that doesn't bother me except when I'm thinking about David or his parents or just what went on there those last awful moments. But I can't bike past there. I see the police cars and the crowds and the barricades when I do. Another thing I'm allergic to.

"Okay," I said. "I'll see a psychologist."

I could see Dad relax. "We've spoken to Dr. Goldstein," he said. "He recommends a man named Dr. Collins. He's in his early thirties and apparently he has an excellent rapport with adolescents."

I disliked him already. He sounded too much like Mr. Glick. "Fine," I said. "Do I set up the appointment or do you?"

"We will," Mom said. "Honey, I'm very proud of you."

"Why?" I asked.

"Because you're behaving so maturely. It isn't always easy to admit you need help."

At this point it's hard not to admit it. So tomorrow one of them is going to call this Collins person, and then mental health, here I come. Besides, maybe seeing a shrink will help me remember what David said to me.

October 25

I went to the hospital after school today to visit with Annie. I've been meaning to for a long time now, but today was the first day I felt I could cope with somebody else's pain. She was in a body cast, and I noticed how much weight she's lost since the accident. Her face was really gaunt.

"How're things going?" I asked. Classic dumb question.

"As well as can be expected," she said. Classic dumb response.

"You've gotten so thin you could be a fashion model when you get out," I said. Thinness is, after all, desirable.

"I know," she said. "The doctors say I'm going to be hell on wheels when they finally spring me."

My face must have been one fine combination of horror and misery, since Annie began giggling. "It's just an expression," she said. "I'm going to walk out of here one of these days."

"Really?" I said.

"Yeah," she said. "There's definitely sensation in my legs. The doctors go around pricking and prodding my feet, and I feel each prick and prod. It's going to take awhile, and there's going to be a lot of physical therapy involved, but I'll be walking again."

"That's wonderful," I said. It was the best news I'd heard in months. "Are you going to be able to graduate with us?"

"I'm doing my best," she said. "But it isn't easy taking exams from this position."

"Of course not," I said. "God might write the answers on the ceiling and then you could cheat."

She laughed. "I'm glad you came," she said. "Lately I haven't had too many visitors."

"Consider yourself lucky," I said. "The way we've all been lately, you're better off not seeing us."

"Jeffrey was here for a couple of days," she said. "I didn't see him, of course, but my parents ran into his parents a few times."

"Do you know how he is?" I asked.

"All I know is he's in a very good sanitarium," she said. "They mostly work with disturbed adolescents. But nobody's too sure it'll do much good."

"Jeffrey was pretty disturbed even before all this began," I said.

"Yeah," she said. "Still."

"Hey," I said. "I'm officially one of those disturbed adolescents myself. Or I'm going to be starting next week. I'm going to see a therapist."

"Really?" Annie asked. "Who? Why?"

"I've been shaky since David died," I said. "Not Jeffrey-level shaky, but upset. You can imagine. The guy's name is Collins."

"Oh, Dr. Collins," Annie said. "He's good. Judd saw him after the accident."

"Really?" I asked. "I didn't know that."

"I probably shouldn't tell you," she said. "Not that it's anything to be ashamed of. Judd blamed himself for the accident, even though it wasn't his fault, and he certainly suffered too. But he felt guilty. He'd call me every day and twice he said that when I was out of the hospital, we'd get married. It had only been our second date. I like Judd, and I appreciated the calls, but I sure wasn't about to marry him. Dr. Collins helped him work out a lot of the guilt."

"Has he withdrawn the proposal?"

"I suppose so," Annie said. "In any event, he calls a lot less often, and when he does, he isn't so god-awful serious anymore. The quantity is down but the quality's improved."

We sat there silently for a couple of minutes.

"Are you thinking the same thing I'm thinking?" Annie asked.

"Probably," I said.

"I was thinking that the last time you came, David came with you," she said.

"That's what I was thinking," I said. "But David didn't come with me. It was his idea to come, so I came with him."

"That sounds right," she said. "David used to visit me regularly twice a week. Tuesday and Friday."

"He never was a spontaneous person," I said.

"No," she said. "But it never seemed pathological. You knew if David made a commitment, you could count on it. After three weeks, I knew he'd be here Tuesday and Friday. And the once or twice he couldn't make it, he called me to let me know."

I realized again how very much I missed David. The feelings took my breath away, but I don't think Annie noticed.

"I used to believe in God," she said. "And in heaven and hell."

"Really?" I said.

"Not anymore though," she said. "After the accident, I stopped believing in God. It seemed pointless praying to somebody who could do this to me. I was real bitter in those days though, and I kept believing in a hell, so I could picture that lousy miserable driver rotting there, suffering all the agonies I was suffering. The pain, the uncertainty, the discomfort. It gave me pleasure to picture him there, even though I never knew what he looked like."

"It must have been horrible," I said.

"It was," she said. "But that's not my point. Maybe I'm just getting softer now that I'm getting better, now that I know I'm not going to spend the rest of my life in a wheelchair, but I don't believe in hell anymore. I don't think I ever really believed in heaven, but I've thrown hell out of my own personal theology.

"You see," she said, looking at me as directly as she could. "I couldn't bear the thought of David there. His life must have been hell enough. He shouldn't have to suffer any more than he already did.

"All I wish for him, for all of us, I suppose, but for David most of all, is peace. That's all. Just simple peace."

October 27

It's been a full month since David died. Just a month. It feels like a decade. Make that a millennium.

October 28

Dad came home in an unbelievable rage tonight. It's Mom's late night at the gallery, so I was the only one around to cope with his mood.

"What's the matter?" I asked. There was no point avoiding the question.

"Those bastards," he said, and he flung this week's *Newsweek* on to the coffee table. "Goddamn the goddamn freedom of the press."

I picked up the *Newsweek* gingerly. "What?" I asked.

"Page 92," he said. "It's a back of the book article."

So I opened it up to page 92, and there was an article there about the traumas of adoption. And on page 93, in one of their short-boxed pieces was a short merciless write-up about David. How he was bitter about being adopted, the fights with his parents. Well behaved at school, rebellious at home. And then the murders and the suicide.

"Why?" I asked. "Why drag it out again?"

"Don't ask me," he said. "I'm just the faithful family retainer."

The Morris estate remains in a state of shambles, and Dad's getting more and more bitter about it. Different family members keep calling him making different demands. At one point last week Dad stared at Mom and me and announced that for our future peace of mind, he was going to leave his entire estate to the Salvation Army.

I couldn't bear having David's face staring at me, and I closed the magazine. "Things were just quieting down," I said. "And they had to rake it all up again."

"Scandalmongering," Dad said. "Pure and simple. Exploit a little tragedy, sell a few more copies. It sickens me."

"Does Mom know?" I asked.

"Not that I know of," he said. "I didn't discover it until I was on the train coming home tonight."

"Maybe we shouldn't tell her," I said.

"She'll find out," he said. "For all we know, she knows already. The gallery's probably been full of talk about the article all day."

"It isn't fair," I said.

"Ain't that the truth," Dad said. "Ain't that the goddamn bloody awful truth."

October 31

Things were buzzing at school today, but not exclusively about the *Newsweek* piece.

We have a new student. His name is Bill something or another, and he's taken David's seat in English.

All this is very unusual. First of all, there usually aren't new seniors; parents generally stick it out for the final year, and then move. Or the kid stays behind with friends to finish school where he began. And new kids coming in at the end of October are weird too. Again, the parents move in the summer or not at all.

And the final strange thing is that this kid came in practically in the middle of the school year, and in his senior year at that and got plopped right into honors English, history, and math (I know about the English and history, because he's in them with me. The math Steffi told me about).

Anyway, this Bill whoever he is, seems very relaxed and at ease with his situation. Maybe he's moved

around a lot before. He certainly didn't seem shy. Mr.
Glick told him to sit there, and once he did, he
started talking to the kids sitting near him. In history,
where he also took David's seat, he did the same.
This time I was one of the kids, but I didn't have
much of a chance to talk with him, since I got questioned three times as hard about things that are involved with David, and I was therefore expected to
tell people everything I knew about the *Newsweek* article (which, of course, was no more than anybody
else knew).

I think it's good there's somebody new around. We
can use some new blood (the vampire approach to
catastrophe).

Later tonight—in lieu of a letter to Jimmy.

Tonight is Halloween, a holiday I haven't cared
about since I was about seven. But for some reason it
got to me more than I expected it to. Maybe it's the
haunted, all hallows' eve, death aspect. Or maybe it's
because David and I used to go trick or treating together when we were kids. We'd fight over handouts,
and make elaborate trades (two Tootsie Rolls for a
bag of M&M's plus one sour ball). I guess without ever
thinking about it, I've come to associate Halloween
with David.

I miss him so much.

November 1

Sometime last night, probably as a Halloween prank, kids (they think) went to the Morris house, broke windows, and threw paint at it. The house looks awful.

The Squabblers (as Dad has taken to calling the various possible Morris family heirs) called Dad all day long to ask him how he could let such a horrible thing happen to what is, approximately, a two-hundred-and-fifty-thousand-dollar house. Dad's been grumbling ever since he came home that he never knew one of the duties of a faithful family retainer was standing guard on empty houses.

It's going to take forever for the estate to be settled, and nobody can sell the house until it is. Mom says that's probably all for the best; she doesn't think many people will want to buy the house with the murders still fresh in people's minds.

I keep feeling I should have woken up last night and heard the glass being broken, so I could have seen who did it. It is possible I did hear the breaking glass, and that's why I woke up. I've been sleeping so miserably, though, I don't need an excuse to wake up.

Why can't people leave the Morrises alone?

November 2

I am now officially on the road to normality.

Luckily for him, Dr. Collins looks nothing like Mr. Glick. He (Collins, that is) is pudgy and sweet-looking. His office looks sort of like Dad's den, nothing threatening about it. We sat in comfortable chairs, facing each other on a diagonal.

"I'm here because my parents think it's a good idea," I said to him after a couple of minutes of introduction and silence.

"Do you think it's a good idea?" he asked.

"Probably," I said. "But I wouldn't have suggested coming on my own."

"I spoke to your parents," he said. "They told me you've been very upset since the Morris incident."

"David was my friend," I said.

"I think I should make one thing clear to you," he said. "I will be seeing you, not your parents. What you tell me is in utter confidence. I will never tell your parents, or anybody else, anything that you tell me, unless you specifically instruct me to. And I suggest strongly that you not tell people what we talk about here."

"Why not?" I asked.

"It impedes progress," he said. "It turns a doctor-patient relationship into a gossip session. Other people's opinions will interfere."

I was glad to hear that. I'd been a little concerned that Mom and Dad would be getting reports. And I really didn't want to sit around at lunch, confessing all. Knowing it was just him and me, helped me relax. And trust him, just a little.

"There is something," I said. "Actually, there's a whole list of somethings, but most of them I figure I can either handle or they'll go away on their own. The day David died, we had lunch together. Just the two of us that day. And we talked all throughout lunch period, but I can't remember anything he told me. I spend hours at night trying to remember, but it never comes back. I can see him, but I can't remember a single, blessed word. And I keep thinking it must be important. Maybe he told me something I could have interpreted. I don't think he said he was going to kill his parents that evening, but I knew David awfully well, and maybe I could have understood something was really wrong. Only I can't remember. I dream about it all the time, horrible dreams where I can see him but I can't hear him."

"That must be very upsetting," he said.

"Of course it's upsetting," I said, sharply.

"You say you can remember what he looked like," Dr. Collins said. "What do you mean? You remember the clothes he was wearing?"

I nodded. "Blue shirt, blue jeans," I said. "A belt I gave him for his birthday last year."

"Do you remember what his face looked like?" Dr. Collins asked. "Was he smiling? Did he seem angry, or upset?"

The image of David entered my mind, as tantalizing and incomplete as ever. "I don't know," I said, closing my eyes to try and see him better. "His face is a blank."

"Do you remember how you felt after lunch?" he asked.

It's funny, I've been concentrating so hard on my memories of David, I haven't been trying to remember me at all. I tried to think back to that day, to the still innocent afternoon.

"I was disturbed," I said. "Something was bothering me."

"Are you sure of that?" he asked. "It would be very easy to assume you were disturbed. Hindsight can be very deceptive."

"No, something was bothering me," I said. "I remember at supper that night—I had supper at my friend Steffi's house—I told her something had been bothering me all day, but I couldn't quite figure out what or why. It must have been what David said to me."

"Not necessarily," he said. "If it had been bothering you all day, it might have been something that happened that morning, something that had nothing to do with David at all."

I concentrated on what had happened that morning. I could remember nothing out of the ordinary. "I don't think so," I said. "I think it must have been David. You have to understand. I knew him. Really knew him. We'd been friends since we were four. There were things he told me he never told anybody else. And there were things he didn't have to tell me since I understood without him saying anything."

"Do you think you could have kept David from killing his parents?" Dr. Collins asked.

Classic questions I've been trying to avoid. "Yeah," I said. "I really do."

"How?"

"I don't know," I said slowly. "I know what I couldn't have done. I couldn't have wrestled the gun away from him, or called Bob and Lorraine and warned them to get out, or used my psychic powers to dissuade him. None of that. But there would have been something."

"If you had known, what would you have done?" Dr. Collins asked. "If David had told you what he was planning to do, would you have believed him? Would you have told his parents? Or your parents?"

"You don't think I could have stopped him, do you?" I asked.

"I don't know you," he said. "I don't know what you're capable of doing."

"I don't know if I would have believed him," I said. "It would have depended on how he said it. I could read David. He could never lie to me."

"It's very hard to control the actions of another person," Dr. Collins said. "And it's almost impossible to control the actions of somebody who is no longer rational."

"But what if I could have?" I asked. "What if I'm right and David did tell me something that I should have been able to understand? What if he told it to me just because he knew how well I knew him, and he wanted me to guess, to figure it out and stop him?" My voice was quivering, and I could feel myself getting ready to cry. That was the last thing I wanted to do just then, cry in front of a stranger.

Dr. Collins handed me a box of tissues. I grabbed a handful.

"There are a lot of what ifs in life," he said. "What if I take French instead of Spanish? What if I go out with John instead of Joe? What if I order a hamburger for lunch and not a hot dog? Life is a matter of choices and for every choice made there's a what if created.

"You can spend your life pursuing the what ifs," he said. "And there are people who do. But I think it's more fruitful to live your life accepting the consequences of your actions, of your choices, than chasing the might have beens."

I wondered if he'd ever said that to Judd. His life must have been filled with what ifs, especially before they learned that Annie would be okay.

"What you're saying makes sense," I said. "And I can see where you're right, when other people are concerned. But I still can't help feeling responsible. I can't help feeling guilty. Maybe it's pointless for me to say it, to feel it, but I should have been there. I should have known. I should have understood what David was saying to me."

"One of the more gratifying things about guilt is that it makes us feel important," Dr. Collins said. "It gives us the center stage."

"Do you think I like feeling like this?" I said. "Are you crazy? I can't sleep. I cry all the time. I get the shakes every time I go near the cafeteria, and the one time I went in, I thought they were going to have to carry me out. You think that's fun?"

"No, of course not," he said.

I felt a brief moment of triumph.

"You're smirking," he said. "Are you aware of that?"

I nodded. He smiled.

"What do you hope to get out of this?" he asked me. "Our sessions together. What are your aims?"

I stopped smirking. "I feel weighed down," I said finally. "Horribly weighed down. I want the weights to be lifted."

"All right," he said. "So why don't you tell me a little about yourself. What you like to do. Who you are. I'd like to know . . ."

Next session is Friday, same time. Wouldn't it be wonderful if it worked? My memory back, my nightmares gone. Maybe it's premature but I can't help smiling.

November 4

So last night I dreamt that David knocked on my door, our old secret knock (two short raps, one long) and I opened the door, and he was dressed in his blue shirt and blue jeans, and he handed me a note that said, "You should have known. You should have heard me."

I woke up crying and cried for over an hour. It felt like I would never smile again.

November 5

Today I told Tracy I was in therapy. She said four other kids had told her the same thing in the past three weeks.

I guess, between David and Jeffrey, there are a lot of jittery parents around here.

Tracy, naturally, refused to tell me who the other four kids were, but she said they were all seeing Dr. Collins (who must really be raking it in). I can make a couple of educated guesses about who's in therapy, but I'd love to know for sure. We could form our own little club.

It's funny that I told Tracy and not Steffi. Part of it is because Tracy is so eminently tellable to, which is why everybody else told her too. But that doesn't explain why I didn't tell Steffi. That's more complicated and has to do with my feelings toward her, which are still very mixed up.

I'm still cool to her. I know she's confused about it, which is perfectly logical, since I'm confused too. After going into the cafeteria with her, she thought— and I guess I did too—that all the bad feeling would end. One of those fine dramatic resolutions, like they have on TV.

But it didn't, and even though I keep telling myself it's silly to hold it against her about the *Times*—I don't act so coolly to the other kids who talked to the reporter, after all—but I guess I still do.

And I know it's crazy, but sometimes I feel like it's her fault I wasn't there for David. If I hadn't had dinner at her house that night, maybe things would be different. My head knows that's dumb, but sometimes I think it anyway.

There are times when I'm so miserable I can almost understand why David killed himself. Not the rest of it, but that one thing makes sense. Not that I'm about to. Just that I understand.

I only wish I had understood before it all happened.

I had a second session with Collins this afternoon (before who? after who?). I told him all about Jeffrey and how much that scared me.

Mom ran into Jeffrey's mother the other day. He's severely depressed, and they don't really expect any improvement for a while.

Poor everybody.

November 7

The new kid is named Bill Newman, and his father is some kind of business executive who got promoted to New York. Bill made a point of joining me for lunch at Juniors today.

I was with Judd and Tracy, trying to work my nerve up to tell Judd that I was seeing Collins too, when Bill came over. He really is very good-looking. He asked if he could join us, and we said certainly, so he did. There went my chance to swap notes with Judd.

"Don't you guys have any fun around here?" he asked after he sat down. "I haven't been here that long, I know, but I've noticed nobody mentions any parties, and nobody seems to be dating much, and I can hardly tell if you even have a football team."

"It's been a rough year," Judd said.

"Bill's right," Tracy said. "I don't think there's been a party since David died."

"I don't think anybody's really been in the mood for one," I said.

"David," Bill said. "I hear his name occasionally,

but I haven't quite figured out the story yet. Who is he anyway?"

"David was a friend of ours," I said. "He died in September."

"Oh," Bill said. "That's rough."

"Yes, it is," I said sharply. I still can't deal with casual questions. "It's been very rough for a lot of us."

"David's best friend had a breakdown afterward," Judd said. "In English class. We were all there. I think in a way that's been even harder to handle than David."

"Wow," Bill said. "No wonder everybody's so down."

"We used to have parties," Tracy said. "Last year we had lots of parties. And this year we were going to have even more because so many more kids have their driver's licenses."

"Maybe I'll give one," Bill said. "Give me a chance to get to know everyone better. What do you think, Lynn?"

"I don't know," I said. I'm one fast thinker these days.

"I think it's a great idea," Tracy said in a no-nonsense voice. "We could use a party to get us out of this mood."

"Great," Bill said. "Lynn, could you help me out with the details?"

I stared at him.

"We could work out the details over the weekend," he continued. "Saturday night maybe. How does that sound?"

It took me a moment to realize he was asking me

out for a date. And then it took me another moment to realize how good that sounded.

"Great," I said. "That sounds great."

"Great," Bill said. "We'll go to the movies first."

"Will that give you guys time to discuss the party?" Judd teased.

"There'll be time," Bill said. "Unless you people are accustomed to big elaborate things."

"Don't worry," Tracy said. "We're used to simple little things. Nothing elaborate."

"Oh, yeah," Judd said. "Like Sandy Bloomburg's sweet sixteen."

So then we started laughing, and we told Bill all the gory details about Sandy's party. And soon he was telling us about the kids he knew from the various schools he'd gone to. And when we walked back to school, Bill walked by my side and asked questions about me. What I liked to do, what college I was applying to. Normal boy/girl questions.

And it felt really good.

November 9

I told Dr. Collins all about my upcoming date and party, and he thought it all sounded fine.

It does too. It's amazing how excited I am about a simple ordinary first date. I guess because it feels like my first date ever.

And then after the date a party. I'll become a social human being yet.

November 10

In an effort to get the Morris estate in some kind of order, the Squabblers asked Dad to go over to their house (windows boarded up, paint blotches still there) and go through Bob and Lorraine's papers.

He's been going there after work for the past couple of days, making inventories of the valuables, things like that. It hasn't been easy on him. He sets his shoulders as he leaves, and he walks with a hunched-over determination. When he comes home, he's pretty silent.

Today, after he came back, he called me into his den. I'd been writing down phone numbers for Bill to call and was glad for the interruption.

"You know I've been going over the Morris papers," he said after I sat down.

I nodded.

"I didn't have the combination to their home safe until yesterday," Dad said, "I found it in their safe deposit box. So today I opened the safe to check out what was in there. Stock certificates, bonds, papers, that sort of thing. I was going to make out a list of all the items. And jewelry. Lorraine kept her valuable jewelry in there."

"Yeah?" I said.

Dad rubbed the back of his neck with his hand. "I found something I wasn't expecting in the safe," he said. "Actually, it's something I don't quite know what to do with. It seems David made out a will and left it in the safe. I don't know how he learned the combination."

"A will?" I said. "Is it legal?"

"It wouldn't hold up in a court of law, no," Dad said. "David was only seventeen when he made it out, and it wasn't witnessed. But the Squabblers might be willing to honor it, although frankly I doubt it."

"When did he make it out?" I asked.

Dad pursed his lips. "The day before he died."

"Oh, no," I said. "Oh God. He must have known then."

"I would think so, yes," Dad said. "It might have been a coincidence, or maybe making the will out gave him the idea, but I doubt it. I'm sure he knew."

I felt that weak, short-of-breath feeling that I've come to know lately. "He didn't say anything in it, did he?" I asked. "About imminent death?"

"No," Dad said. "He made a couple of simple bequests, that's all."

"I wonder how long he knew," I said. "How long he'd been planning."

"We'll never know," Dad said.

"The bequests," I said. "What were they?"

"He left his cameras, all his photographic equipment, and his books to Jeffrey," Dad said. "To Mom and me, he left that pen-and-ink sketch he bought at the gallery last year."

"That was nice of him," I said, then realized how foolish my words sounded. It was nice of someone who was planning a double murder and suicide to leave my parents a remembrance. I grimaced.

Dad ignored me. "He left you his guitar and his notebooks," he said.

"What?" I said.

"I assume he meant the guitar you have anyway," Dad said. "I admit I'm puzzled by the notebooks. Do you know anything about them?"

"No," I said. "Do you think it was some kind of diary?"

"I really don't know," Dad said. "I haven't found it going through his parents' papers."

"Maybe he destroyed them," I said. "No, that

doesn't make sense, does it? That he'd mention them one day and destroy them the next. He must have hidden them somewhere."

"Probably," Dad said. "The police went over the house in September, but since they had David's confession, they probably didn't look too hard for anything else."

"What are you going to do with the will?" I asked.

"It's evidence," Dad said. "So I figured I'd tell Lieutenant Donovan about it."

"Do you have to tell him about the notebooks?"

"Yes," Dad said. The question was obviously not open to discussion.

I sighed. "He won't understand," I said.

"He may not even care," Dad said. "But I have an obligation to tell him. I'm going to call him tomorrow morning."

"Are you going to tell Jeffrey's parents?" I asked.

"I really don't know," Dad said. "They've suffered so much already, and the will isn't legally binding. I think I'll wait to see what the Squabblers say, Jeffrey doesn't need David's things right now, after all."

"Should I go to the house and look for David's notebooks?" I almost hoped Dad would say no.

"We'll see what Lieutenant Donovan says," Dad said. "If he doesn't object, I'll go with you. But it's up to him."

I agreed and left the room. David wrote notebooks and left them to me. I'm glad he didn't leave them to Jeffrey. Maybe it's sick of me, but I take pride in the fact that David trusted me to read his private thoughts.

Assuming the notebooks are his private thoughts.

They might just be notes from last year's history and English and math classes. I guess I won't know until I know what Donovan says.

November 11

Donovan said that he was already involved in another case, and that David's file was officially closed. He would like to see a copy of the will, however (Dad promised to send him a photostat), and if we located the notebooks, he'd appreciate the chance to read them.

So now there's nothing stopping me from going to the Morris house and looking until I find them. Somehow, I'm not in a rush.

I didn't want to tell Dr. Collins about the notebooks, not until I know what's in them, so I told him about my nightmares. Fortunately, I continue to have enough of them to fill up any fifty-minute hour.

November 12

An awful day. The worst, I think, since Jeffrey broke down.

Things started out fine. I was looking forward to my date with Bill. The way I haven't looked forward to anything in a long time. A real old-fashioned date. And I like Bill too. The evening sounded like it would be fun.

Everything would have been fine, I think, if Dad hadn't asked me to go with him to the Morris house to look for David's notebooks. I was feeling just good and just dumb enough to agree to go. So I put on my jacket and went with him. Only I hadn't counted on how I'd feel actually going through the door. I haven't been there since it all happened. Sure I've passed the house, and I look down at it every night before I go to bed, but that's not the same as actually going in. Of course I had Dad with me, which should have helped. It probably did, since I was so weak kneed by the time we actually got to the front door that I don't think I could have entered if I'd been alone.

But Dad just unlocked the door, like it was the

most natural thing in the world to do, and I followed him in.

It was the most overwhelming sensation going in there. I honestly think my heart stopped beating for a moment. I had a brief flash of every thought and feeling I'd ever had about Bob and Lorraine and David. The good times, the bad, all of it came over me. I could feel their presence there, not like ghosts, but just overwhelming memories. Bob drinking his Scotch and sodas. Lorraine cheerfully talking about the most intimate part of her life. And David . . . So many images of David, pacing, lying down on the sofa, shoes deliberately kept on, sitting quietly in a corner, pretending not to be there. I walked into the living room and sat down, only because I had to sit down, or else I would have fainted.

"Do you want to check David's room?" Dad asked.

The last place in the world I wanted to be was in David's room, but I knew I'd have to do it sometime. So I climbed the stairs (I'm still not sure how; my legs felt like they were made of iron) and went in.

The police had obviously been through the room, and equally obviously, no one had straightened up after them. I felt a little better than I would have otherwise, since David always kept his room so immaculate. With it messy, it didn't feel quite so strongly his, and I was able to go in.

But I couldn't look through his things. I just couldn't. I tried, to the extent of picking up a couple of things off his desk, opening his closet door, and checking out titles of books on his shelves, But none of that was serious-looking. If David's notebooks were a real journal, he would have kept it well concealed, and I didn't have the heart or stomach to look. I

stood there for a few minutes, then started straighten-
ing things out. I did it mindlessly, just put loose papers in piles, that kind of thing, but when I was
finished, the room looked a lot neater. That of course
was a big mistake since it looked more like David
once I was finished. So as soon as I got shaky again,
I ran downstairs, found Dad, and told him that I
hadn't been able to find David's notebooks, and
I really didn't have any more time to look, and ran
across the street to the safety of my own house. I
nearly got run over too, since I didn't look when
I was crossing, and there was a car driving by.

Once home I made it to my bedroom, where after I
stopped shaking, I started crying. I don't have moods
of missing David often, but when they do occur, I'm
absolutely helpless. I think about all the things we
shared, and the realization that he is gone, done, finished, no longer existing comes as a fresh hard shock
all over again. It's like I've divided his dying and his
death. Most of my energies have gone into accepting
the facts of his dying. The fact of his death is separate, and I don't seem to believe it quite as much.
But seeing his room so empty, yet so David, really got
to me. I miss him so much.

I thought about calling Bill and postponing our
date, but I honestly thought if I did something, got
out of my house and my thoughts, I'd feel better for
it. So I showered and washed my hair and put on
fresh clothes. I thought about everything except
David, and I really was feeling better by the time Bill
arrived.

We went to the movies and saw some silly comedy,
which was in spite of (or perhaps because of) its idi-
ocy, very funny. From there we joined some of the

kids, and went to Juniors for ice cream sundaes. Around midnight we decided to go home, so Bill drove me back here. Up till then everything was fine, I hadn't felt so happy in a long time.

Bill parked the car in front of the house, and we sat still for a few moments enjoying the warmth of the car, the song on the radio, and the quiet of the street. Then he leaned over to kiss me.

I certainly wasn't surprised when he did. But even though I knew he was going to, and I wanted him to, for that matter, I jumped from him like he'd given me an electric shock.

"What?" he asked.

"I'm sorry," I said. "Really. Please."

"Please what?"

"Please kiss me."

He gave me a funny look. Boy, am I getting used to funny looks.

"Well?" I asked.

"Well what?"

"Well, aren't you going to kiss me?"

"No," he said. "Not if you're going to have that attitude toward it."

"What attitude?" I asked belligerently.

"Forget it," he said, looking away from me.

"I will not," I said. "What attitude?"

"I like to kiss girls who like to be kissed," Bill said. "Not girls who jump away, then apologize, then act like they're doing me a favor letting me kiss them."

"I didn't mean to sound like that," I said. "I didn't even mean to jump."

"Then why did you?"

"I don't know," I said. "Dammit, can't we forget it all happened, and just start all over again."

"All right," he said, and leaned over me. We kissed. Nothing.

"Great," he said.

"I'm sorry," I said.

"Don't apologize all the time," he said. "That isn't helping matters any."

"I'm out of practice," I said. "I haven't dated anyone since David died. Not that I dated David . . . But I just haven't felt like going out since then."

"You don't forget how to kiss," he said. "It's like riding a bicycle."

I giggled nervously.

"Look," Bill said, and then he was silent. "I know you cared very deeply about David."

I sat there, waiting for the lecture. At this point I could recite it myself. It's about time you started living again. You can't let David's memory destroy your life. David is dead and you have to accept it. All that.

But Bill surprised me. "You're not ready yet," he said. "You're still in mourning."

"Yes," I said.

"Some things don't go away as easily as you think they ought to," he said.

I nodded. I only hoped things would someday really go away.

"It's only November," he said. "What's that been, less than two months? That's not very long at all. It's just people get impatient with other people's grief."

"Grief does end, doesn't it?" I asked.

"It does," he said. "Maybe it never disappears, but it melts away into something more manageable. We have time."

"Oh, Bill," I said.

"But you'd better mean it when you say you're

ready," he said, running his fingers through his hair. "I can't handle being a yo-yo. Back and forth, up and down. I'd rather wait and not see you than see you and go through another ten minutes like this."

"I'll be honest," I said.

He smiled. "That's quite a promise," he said. "But I'm going to hold you to it. Now go home and start recovering. And unless I hear otherwise, I'll assume we're still planning my party together."

I kissed him lightly and ran out of the car and into the house. He waited until I was safely inside before he left. Mom and Dad blessedly were in bed, so I went straight up to my room and cried some more. Maybe I shouldn't have. Maybe I should feel good there's somebody who understands. But I cried anyway.

November 13

I spent the day nursing a headache. It came from trying to figure out where David's notebooks are. The more I thought about it, the more my head hurt. I took a half a bottle of aspirin, all together, and cursed a lot in my mind.

November 16

I didn't want to discuss my date with Bill with Dr. Collins, since I feel like an idiot about the whole thing. Besides, I hadn't been able to figure out where David left his notebooks, and that's been driving me crazy. So I told Dr. Collins about the will and the notebooks instead.

"David sure didn't want you to forget him," he said.

"What?" I said.

"Leaving you his notebooks," Dr. Collins said.

"I'm glad David left them to me," I said. "That shows he trusted me. I just wish I could figure out where he put them."

"One reason David chose you to receive his notebooks is because he knew you'd know where to find them," Dr. Collins said.

"I suppose," I said.

"Where did he usually hide things?"

"All over the place," I said. "David hid everything at some point in his life. He didn't like his parents to know things. Like once he got this 78 on a test..."

"Yes?" Dr. Collins said.

"I'm so stupid," I said, torn between shouting at myself for being so dumb, and hugging myself for finally being so smart. "Things that were really secret David hid at my house. That way he'd be sure his parents would never find them, but he'd have access to them. Bad test grades, girly magazines, all kinds of crap. He won a photography contest once, and he hid the letter of congratulations in our attic. His parents didn't like him to waste his time taking pictures. The notebooks are probably there. It would have been easy enough for him to put them there; he had a key to our house. I'll check as soon as I get in."

"You know, Lynn, even if you do find the notebooks, you're under no obligation to read them," Dr. Collins said.

"Of course I'll read them," I said. "David wanted me to."

"Did you always do what David wanted you to?" he asked.

"No, of course not," I said impatiently. "But I don't see why I shouldn't read them."

"At some point you're going to have to put David away," Dr. Collins said. "You'll want to go on with your own life."

I thought about Bill and I blushed. "I'm not ready yet," I said. "I'll know when I am, and then I'll forget all about David. Will that satisfy you?"

"I don't expect you to forget about David," Dr. Collins said. "But I do think you'll be happier when you no longer use him as a reason for everything you do."

"I don't do that," I said. "Besides, if I don't read the notebooks, I'll always wonder if I should have. You know that."

"Yes, I suppose I do," Dr. Collins said.

I can't convince Dr. Collins of things too often, so I felt good that I'd gotten him to agree with me. I was feeling overall good anyway, just knowing I was going to find the notebooks when I got home. So as soon as my session was over, I ran home, feeling freer than I have in a long time. I love running. That's something I haven't done enough of lately.

The house was empty, so I let myself in and went straight to the attic. I practically flew up the stairs. I knew just where to go, to David's private corner. I'd found his test paper with its 78 there by accident once, and David had been furious with me, even though it was my attic and not his. He made me swear I'd never tell anyone that was his special hiding place, and I would never look for things there either. He really did trust me, and I lived up to his trust. Sometimes he'd show me things before he hid them, but I never looked. Not until today.

And there David's secrets were, waiting for me. Some contact sheets, some sheet music for his guitar, an English paper from last year with a note from the teacher saying "David, you can do much better than this" and a C+ written in red, and four spiral notebooks.

The minute I saw them, I thought about what Dr. Collins had said about how I didn't have to read them. I didn't even want to touch them. The only David I could remember then was the one who was responsible for so much death. But then I thought about the David I loved, and I knew the notebooks were from him. So I put the other stuff back and took the notebooks downstairs to my bedroom.

Even then I didn't really want to start reading.

The notebooks were musty and had an attic smell to them, like they were very old, but I knew they had to be fairly recent. I could remember when David started buying that sort of notebook—it was at the start of sophomore year. He liked the way they looked, he said, the way they felt in his hands. All notebooks looked the same to me, but David thought these were special.

I got a tissue and wiped the dust off them. That forced me to look at them. I could see David had numbered each one. And on the fourth one he had written, "Lynn, you'll understand."

So I knew I had to read them. But not just yet.

November 18

I told Dr. Collins I found the notebooks and was going to start reading them tonight. He just nodded.

So after supper, I went to my bedroom, closed the door (I haven't told Mom and Dad yet about the notebooks. I'm waiting to see what David wrote), took out notebook number one and opened it. My hands were really shaking, and for a moment I couldn't get my eyes to focus. But then I looked down, and all there was was David's handwriting, and all it said was, "I had supper with the Epsteins tonight. Afterward Jimmy and I played chess. I wish he was a better player; it's boring beating him all the time."

And I felt like the David I'd lost was back with me, and I stayed up half the night reading and remembering and sharing with David again.

November 19

I got up this morning, gulped down breakfast, and went back upstairs to start reading David's journals again. So the first thing I read was: "I talked to Lynn about Jeffrey today. I think she understands now," and I didn't have the slightest idea what he was talking about. Most of the stuff I remember, but this one stumped me. I stared at that entry for five minutes or so, trying to reconstruct what things were like then. It was our sophomore year. Jeffrey and David had become really close the year before.

I knew I couldn't blame myself for not remembering everything David and I ever talked about, but it bothered me that I couldn't. But then I remembered that that year I tried to keep a diary myself. So I dug out my once precious volume, checked out the date, and sure enough I had written: "David and I had a long talk today about Jeffrey. I still think Jeffrey is crazy, but I can understand a little better why David likes him so much."

And then I remembered. It was February (I started that diary in January and discarded it by March), and so we had just gotten a snow day. There must have been a foot of the stuff outside, when David trudged his way across the street, carrying his guitar, and wearing his camera case around his neck.

I had been bored watching quiz shows and re-runs of *I Love Lucy* and was delighted for the company. Jimmy had the flu and was in bed, complaining that the day he would have taken off from school was a snow day anyway. Dad had stayed in the city the night before. I remember how odd that had felt, and how many conversations he and Mom had had about whether he should try to brave the blizzard to come home. He'd ended up spending the night in his office.

Mom was home, the gallery hadn't bothered to open, and she was busy doing standard American mother things, like making hot chocolate and tending to Jimmy. So David and I were pretty much on our own. He insisted I come outside; he wanted to take pictures of me in the snow. So I made snow angels, and even a snowman that Jimmy could see from his bedroom window. And David kept snapping pictures. He gave prints of a couple of the better shots to Mom and Dad. A lot of the pictures looked overexposed. David said he hadn't accounted for the glare of the sun on the snow.

"I'll never make that mistake again," he'd said, when he brought the prints over.

And I remember feeling a little eerie, as though David kept a list of mistakes, and crossed off the ones he would never make again. I make the same mistakes over and over again. I can never remember that $7 \times 8 = 56$. I always think it's 54. Things like that.

Anyway David finally took enough pictures to satisfy him, and he helped me finish up the snowman and agreed to go into the house. We stomped around in the kitchen, trying to warm up, and Mom gave us some hot chocolate, which we took into the den. We were just getting comfortable when the phone rang.

I answered it. It was Jeffrey. "Is David there?" he asked. "His mother said he might be."

"Jeffrey," I said to David, and scowled.

"Hi Jeffrey," David said. "What can I do for you?"

They talked for close to five minutes, while I sat there, drank my hot chocolate, and felt hostile. Didn't Jeffrey know it was rude to call someone up at someone else's house?

Eventually David hung up. I wasted no time. "That Jeffrey drives me crazy," I said. "Why do you put up with him?"

David didn't blink an eye. Now that I think about it, David was almost never startled. Was he always that wary that nothing caught him by surprise?

"What's wrong with Jeffrey?" he asked.

"He's a creep," I said. "That's what's wrong with him."

"Except for that," David said.

"You admit he's a creep?" I said.

"I can see where if you don't like Jeffrey, you'd think he's a creep," David said. "But I like him, so it doesn't matter to me."

"How can you like him if he's a creep?" I asked.

"He's very smart," David said.

"So am I," I said. "So are a lot of kids in this school. Kids who aren't creeps too."

"Jeffrey's smart in different ways," David said. "He knows about a lot of things you're not interested in. He's the only person I play chess with I consistently lose to."

"And for that he's your best friend?"

"I like playing chess," David said. He had that smug look on his face that used to drive me absolutely crazy.

"There's more to life than chess," I said. "You can't have a best friend just because he can beat you in chess. Don't you talk? Don't you get the creeps talking to him? Doesn't his skin bother you?"

David laughed. "Jeffrey isn't as bad as you make him out," he said. "After all, you aren't as bad as he thinks either."

I wasn't surprised to learn Jeffrey didn't like me, but that didn't make me any happier. "You two talk about me?" I asked nervously.

"Not much," David said. "With Jeffrey I can talk about chess and books and photography. Stuff that doesn't interest you." He was silent for a moment, and then he took his guitar out of its case and started tuning it. "I only have the two of you," he said, not looking up. "Don't put down the only other friend I have, Lynn."

Even then I knew how much it cost him to say that. So I changed the subject, abruptly I'm sure, to geometry, or something equally important. And I did understand a little better. If you have only two friends in the entire world, you can't afford to be fussy about one of them.

And I even felt sorry for Jeffrey, for the first time,

sorry and not disgusted or horrified. He only had David, after all.

Poor Jeffrey. I hope he's getting better. I know how hard it can be.

Later

Bill called me and invited me over to his house to help him make party plans. He's decided to have it in two weeks.

I was halfway through with David's journals and really didn't want to be interrupted, but I could just imagine what Dr. Collins would say about that. So I agreed to go. I biked over and got there around three. I can now bike past the Morris house in the daytime, although I continue to go the long way around at night. Still, it's progress.

Bill and I went over the guest list. Bill pretty much decided to invite everybody. Which made things easier.

"A party will be nice," I said. "We could all use one."

"Things must really have been hard around here," Bill said.

"Hard enough," I said. For the first time in a while, I wasn't feeling bad about things. I was back a year ago with David. When things were safe and normal.

"What exactly happened?" Bill asked.

"What do you mean?" I asked, instantly wary.

"With David," he said. "I've heard a lot of stories, but I don't really believe any of them."

I didn't like being brought back to reality about David.

"He shot his parents," I said coldly. "His father first, and then his mother. And then he killed himself."

I still can't say the words or write them down or think them, without projecting myself into the house during those awful moments. Did Bob understand what David was doing and why? Did he fear for Lorraine as well as himself? Did he even have time for fear, or was it all over for him as soon as it began? Did Lorraine hear the shot? Did she know what had happened when David shot her? Was she thinking about Bob then or herself? Was any of her pain and grief reserved for David? And David himself? Did he pride himself on a job well done, as he went from parent to parent, from slaughter to slaughter? Did he turn the light off before he killed himself to punish himself for what he had done? Or was it a welcoming gesture to death? Did he mourn, even for a moment? Or was he joyous?

"Is that all you know?" Bill asked. "Just the bare facts?"

"His father was upstairs, watching television," I said. "His mother was downstairs, washing the supper dishes. David left the TV set on, but he turned the water off. His mother still had the rubber gloves on her hands, when she died. Is that what you want to hear?"

"No," Bill said. "I'm sorry. It's just that the whole thing has such a morbid fascination to it. Or I feel a morbid fascination. I didn't mean to upset you."

I was crying by that point, so there was no point politely lying and saying I wasn't upset, and he shouldn't feel bad. I grabbed tissues from my pocketbook (I travel with a stack of them now, in case of a crying jag. I do have them when I least expect to).

"Can I get you something to drink?" he asked. "Water or a Coke?"

"I'm okay," I said, blowing my nose, and rubbing the tears off my cheeks. "I'm sorry. I haven't learned how to control my feelings yet."

"Of course not," Bill said. "It was stupid of me."

"It's those goddamn rubber gloves," I said, half laughing, half crying. "They get me every time. Lorraine was always so vain about her hands."

"It must be awful for you," Bill said.

"The pain doesn't seem to want to stop," I said, calming down some more. "I keep hoping it'll go away, but it doesn't."

"I understand," he said. "Pain is like that. You think you're over something, and then all of a sudden it grabs you and because you don't expect it, you can't handle it."

"David was a very good friend of mine," I said, trying to keep my voice under control, trying not to think about the notebooks. "I loved him in a way I don't love my other friends. Maybe because I knew him for so many years. Maybe because I knew him so well. But I don't know why he did it. I can understand, in a big amorphous way, but what drove him that particular day, I don't know. I can't know. Nobody can. As far as I can tell, there was no one thing." I paused for a moment, and wiped away the last tears. "He was very unhappy. He was very unhappy all his life. Can you understand that? There was never a moment of his life, at least none that I know of, where he knew real happiness. It was always watered down with rage or sorrow. Can you imagine what that must have been like?"

"I think I can," Bill said.

"Maybe you can," I said. "Most people can't. I can't always, myself. So people make up stories to explain it to themselves. And it doesn't really matter if the stories have any truth to them, because people can't understand the truth."

"Does it help to talk?" he asked, and started gently massaging the back of my neck.

"A little," I admitted.

"I thought it would," he said. "Boy, you're tense. Those muscles are as tight as a drum. Talking things out might help relax you."

"What makes you so understanding?" I asked him. I almost resented the way he understood me better than I did. Sort of like Dr. Collins, only without all the degrees.

"I don't know," Bill said. "I like understanding people. And I've moved around a lot with my family."

"That doesn't mean you're going to understand people," I said. "It could mean you don't understand anybody, because you've moved around so much you don't have the chance to get to know people."

"Okay, you want to know, I'll tell you," Bill said. "I've made a point of it. You move around, you have to figure out a way of getting people to like you real fast. It can be pretty damn lonely otherwise. So I act interested in people. I mean, I am interested in people, it isn't really an act, but I make my interest obvious. I ask questions. I'm a good listener. I make eye contact."

"Eye contact?"

"I've read books about it," Bill said, slipping his arm around my shoulders. "The right amount of eye contact is very important. It convinces people of your sincerity."

"I don't believe this," I said. "You mean all this sympathy is just an act?"

"I don't mean that at all," Bill said. "I just make sure people learn real fast that I am interested. Then they tell me things. And I really listen. I pay attention. Don't you like it when people pay attention to you?"

Lately people have been paying all kinds of attention to me, and I'm not that crazy about a lot of it. But I knew what Bill meant, so I nodded. I also grinned.

"You must think I'm an awful phony," Bill said. "But I'm not. I really do like understanding what makes people tick. I like listening. I like having people tell me things."

"Like Tracy," I said.

"Yeah," Bill said. "Only I do it hard sell, because I don't have the time to do it any other way. So I come on strong. I practically order people to tell me things."

I turned around and stared at him, half in horror. And then Bill laughed, and I joined him.

"I'm not that bad," he said. "But I guess I am pretty aggressive about it. The thing is, after years of listening to people, I have a pretty good idea of how people act. What they feel. I've heard practically everything. Although I have to admit this business with David is new to me."

"What do you think you're going to do with this

talent of yours?" I asked. "Become a therapist? Or an advice to the lovelorn columnist?"

"Neither," Bill said. "Advertising."

I roared. I can't remember the last time I laughed so hard and so loud.

"You can laugh," Bill said, and started laughing too. "A gift like mine shouldn't go to waste. I'm going to make a fortune in advertising."

Eventually our laughter subsided to giggles. My sides hurt from laughing so much, and God, that felt good.

"I've never told anybody all this," Bill said. He gestured with his free hand, as though to show me the enormity of what he'd just said. "People don't like to think the person who's listening so hard and being so understanding has an ulterior motive."

"No," I said trying hard not to giggle again. "I don't suppose they do."

"Besides, oddly enough, I'm not in the habit of confiding things," Bill said. "You'll keep all this to yourself?"

"Oh, Bill," I said, sorry that I would have to, and sorry that he had to ask. "Of course I will."

"I like your laugh," he said. "You don't laugh enough."

"No," I said. "I don't suppose I do."

I got home around six and I really didn't want to read the journals. I was feeling too good about Bill and the party. So I gave myself the evening off. I'll get back to the notebooks tomorrow. They'll still be there.

November 21

The notebooks can get me into trouble, if I'm not careful. I was having lunch with Steffi, Bill, and Tracy, when I started thinking about the stuff I read yesterday, just a little crack about Steffi, and it was all I could do not to laugh out loud.

"The question for today," David wrote last May, "is whether I should ask Steffi to the Junior Prom. I think not, although it would certainly make her happy enough. But if I don't ask her, she'll find somebody else to go with. And if I do ask her, she'll probably think it's a proposal."

David's journals don't usually make me smile, but I positively giggled at that. Steffi had been chasing after David for years, and for years David had been avoiding her.

Now that I think about it, a lot of the girls had crushes on David at one point or another. I think it was his inaccessibility that was so appealing. David was obviously not about to ask anyone out, so it was safe to have a crush on him. Besides, if you were the one he finally chose, it would be worth so much more than if somebody more socially active asked.

So girls had crushes on him and came to me for advice. But Steffi never got over hers. She fell in love with David the first minute she saw him, which was in eighth grade when she transferred to our school. And she stayed in love with him ever since.

Not that she didn't date other people. Steffi isn't one to sit around on a Saturday night pining. But she would have dropped everyone for David.

It's funny that he knew it. I guess it's natural that he would have, and now that I think about it, he led Steffi on a little. Steffi, for her part, actually got Jeffrey to go on a date with her, hoping beyond hope that David would be jealous. I thought it was more likely he'd step in to try and protect Jeffrey. But David just sat back and enjoyed the spectacle.

"I can't go out with Jeffrey again," Steffi had told me the next day. "I don't care if it costs me David. I just can't. He tried to kiss me last night, and all I could see were those giant pimples. Can you imagine what Jeffrey's skin looks like close up?"

David ended up not going to the Junior Prom last year. Steffi went with Brian Cleary. I went with Mark Schwartz. We both prided ourselves on having seniors as dates. According to Steffi, Brian damn near raped her afterward, but she may have made that up, for me to tell David, to get him concerned. Or maybe aroused. Either way I didn't tell him, so it didn't work. Nothing Steffi ever did worked with David. I know it never would, but I'm glad David enjoyed the attention.

And I know he'd like the idea of my laughing with him, through him, at Steffi and her crush. I guess it's okay to laugh, just as long as Steffi doesn't know I am.

One thing the notebooks aren't doing for me is help me remember what David said to me that last day. I really thought they would, that they'd jar that part of my subconscious I have my memory of that lunch locked up in. But it hasn't happened. The notebooks do make me think about it though.

Actually, the harder I concentrate on it, the fuzzier the images become. Dr. Collins says I shouldn't try too much, that when I'm ready to remember, it'll all come back to me.

The problem is I don't think I'll ever be ready to remember. So I'm trying to hurry the process along and get it over with.

I could ask Steffi if she remembers why I was upset that day, but I don't think I knew then what was bothering me. It was like an itch when you can't see the actual mosquito bite. Just a sensation.

Jimmy called to tell us for sure he'll be home for Thanksgiving. There had been plenty of three-day weekends he could have come in for the past couple of months, but we've made a point of not pushing him to come home.

I haven't spoken to Jimmy since those little 3:00 A.M. sessions I used to have. It's going to be weird to see him again. Weirder for him probably. He's had plenty of time to adjust to the idea, but it's still going to be a shock for him when he sees the Morris house all boarded up. Nobody cut the grass all fall; it looks really ramshackle there.

Oh, well. Maybe if I talk to him about it, I'll be able to remember what David said. Or maybe he has some idea on his own. He didn't leave for college until about a week before it happened. Maybe David talked to him. He did that sometimes, borrowed Jimmy as an older brother.

I wonder if Jimmy's been having nightmares too. Did he have anybody he could talk to at 3:00 A.M.?

November 22

Jimmy's coming in late tomorrow night. I decided that I ought to finish reading David's notebooks before he got home, so they wouldn't be hanging over my head.

I don't know what it is, but the closer I get to the end, the less I want to read the notebooks. So I practically had to force myself tonight and then I was sorry that I did.

Most of David's notebook entries are several pages long. But the more something bothered him, the shorter his entry. It took me a while to figure that pattern out, but now I understand it. So it didn't surprise me just to read "Fight with parents. No sympathy from Epsteins," from last June.

That one was a real killer (great choice of words). I wonder if my parents think about it ever. Not that it was their fault, but David was devastated, and I was furious, and things were tense for a long time.

It's funny. I had to concentrate to remember what David was fighting about with Bob and Lorraine. David wanted to take a photography course in the city that summer, and they didn't want him to. They wanted him to go to one of those survival training courses out west. "David spends too much time inside," Bob said. "Look at him, he's positively scrawny. And he's scared of his own shadow. What kind of man is he going to make, behaving like a sissy all the time?"

Bob and Lorraine wanted David to spend his summers away from home. They packed him off for camp every summer since first grade. He used to run away two or three times a summer, and I know the camps used to finally refuse to take him back, but they always found someplace else. They'd travel a lot during the summer when David was gone.

In the winter Bob and Lorraine were always signing David up for activities that he didn't go to. And then he'd go home and lie to them about it. For two straight years, he had them convinced he was a Boy Scout, until Lorraine ran into the scoutmaster one day and demanded to know why David hadn't earned any merit badges yet.

David's sneaking around bothered my parents a lot more than it bothered Bob and Lorraine. They'd get furious, of course, and David would be punished, but Mom and Dad really worried about it. I think they were a little afraid I'd learn how to be sneaky from him. I'm about as sneaky as a bull elephant, but parents are weird that way.

So Bob and Lorraine announced to David that he was going to be spending that summer in Wyoming learning how to survive in canyons and places like that.

"It's a very exclusive program," they told us one evening. "And it costs a fortune. But it's just the thing for David."

"I'm not going," David told me the next day. "I'll take the plane out to Wyoming, if they have planes out there, and then I'll hitch back to New York and spend the summer in the city. They'll never know."

David had a way of saying "they" that nobody else does. He could put such scorn into that single word.

"Where will you stay?" I asked nervously.

"I don't know," he said. "The Y maybe. And then when they're gone, I'll pop up here. Your parents will take me in. Worse comes to worst, I'll stay at my house until they get back."

"You can't do that," I said. "Hitching can be dangerous. And the people in Wyoming will tell your parents when you don't show up. And then God only knows what your parents will do."

"They won't do anything if they can't find me," David said, looking me straight in the eyes. "And they won't be able to find me if I'm on the road."

"But you'll have to come back here eventually," I said. "Face it, David, you don't want to be a runaway. You want to spend the summer going into New York taking photography courses. On air-conditioned trains."

"So what do you think I should do?" he asked.

"I'll talk to my parents," I said. "No, better yet, we'll both talk to them. Maybe if they tell your parents they think you should take that course, your parents will agree. And you could stay here while they're away. Okay?"

"Okay," David said, so we trotted downstairs and found my parents in the living room. "I was wondering if I could talk to you about something," he said to them.

"Sure," Dad said, looking up from his book. "What is it?"

"You know my parents have this crazy idea about what I should be doing this summer," David said. "The thing is, I refuse to do it."

"David, you really should give their idea a try," Mom said, putting the newspaper down. "You might enjoy it. Besides, think of all the great pictures you could take in Wyoming."

"Wyoming will still be there if I ever want to go," David said. "And the pictures I could take now wouldn't be nearly as good as the ones I'd be able to take after I've had some photography courses."

"Your parents are eager for you to go to this survival course," Dad said.

"I don't see what I need it for," David said, petulantly. "It isn't like I'm going to spend the rest of my life trying to survive in the wilderness. On the subways maybe, but not the wilderness."

"So what do you want us to do?" Mom asked, tapping the newspaper with her finger.

"I want you to tell my parents that I refuse to go," David said. "Tell them I'll run away if they make me."

Even I knew David had just made a tactical error. Dad looked angry. "I have no intention of telling them that," he said. "I don't pass along threats."

"David just thought maybe he could spend the summer here," I said, real fast. "And then he could take his photography course, and Bob and Lorraine could go to London like they want."

"No," Dad said, firmly.

"No?" David said.

"David, you can't use us as a buffer zone with your parents forever," Dad said. "You're sixteen, almost seventeen. At some point you're going to have to learn to deal with your parents directly, without using us. And you can't learn to deal with them by making threats, directly or indirectly. You're going to have to learn to accept them as your parents."

"They're not my parents," David said, looking at Dad coldly.

"That's nonsense," Dad said. "Immature drivel."

"Dad," I said.

"Go home, David, and talk to your parents openly," Dad said. "Tell them you don't want to go to Wyoming. Tell them what your reasons are. Listen to their reasons. And don't hide behind your anger."

"Thank you, sir," David said. He stood very straight, and looked at Dad with ice cold anger. "Now I know just where I stand here."

"We love you, David," Mom said. "But we aren't your parents."

"I never thought you were," he said. "If you'll excuse me, I'll be going now."

"David," I said, but he had already marched out. I watched him cross the street and go home. When I saw him enter the front door, I turned around to face my parents.

"How could you do that?" I cried. "Do you know what he's planning to do if he's sent to Wyoming?"

"That's not our business," Dad said.

"You can't say that," I said. "David's family too.

You know that. What's this business about how he has to learn how to deal with Bob and Lorraine? He can't deal with them. Just because he's sixteen you think suddenly he'll be able to?"

"It's about time he started," Dad said.

"Your father and I thought David might come to us with some idea about this summer," Mom said. "And we talked about inviting David to spend it here. We even talked to Bob and Lorraine about it."

"I can just imagine what they said," I said.

"They said that they would prefer it if we didn't invite David," Mom said. "They feel that, unintentionally, we've been a barrier between them and David. They really do want to be close to him."

"He hates them," I said. I'd never said that out loud, although David had certainly said it often enough to me. It still sounded odd coming from my mouth.

"Teen-agers frequently hate their parents," Dad said. "You've hated us on occasion, no doubt. Do you really think you would've been able to resolve those feelings by running away and staying someplace else?"

"So you're closing the door to David?" I asked angrily. "To force him to make peace with Bob and Lorraine."

"That's the idea," Mom said. "We all decided upon it."

"It isn't going to work," I said. It's funny how much I knew that.

I was right, of course, in the short run, as well as the long. David had another fight with his parents, and ended up spending three days at Jeffrey's. By that point Lorraine was in tears begging Mom to take

David back in, if he should ask, because she really
hated Jeffrey's parents, and couldn't deal with them
at all. So David moved in here for a week or so. Bob
and Lorraine made no effort to contact him once he
was here; they ran into him on the street, and they
barely nodded. David warmed back up to my parents
though. I guess he figured he had won. David could
be very generous in victory.

As it happened, David didn't do anything last summer. The survival course turned him down after he
went into New York for an interview. And the photography course he wanted was cancelled because not
enough people signed up for it.

So David spent the summer reading books and
playing his guitar and taking pictures on his own.
Bob and Lorraine went to London, and David stayed
with us. He was pretty happy, for David.

Jimmy is just going to have to put up with me dis-
tracted. I can't finish the notebooks before he gets
back. Over the weekend I'll have plenty of time, and
I'll finish them then.

November 27

I spent as much of the weekend as I could with Jimmy. Dad and Mom wanted to see him too, so I had to share his attentions, but Jimmy and I stayed up after they went to bed and talked until two or three in the morning.

A lot of what we talked about was just fun stuff—movies he's seen, people he's met, and things he's learned. I in turn told him about the lighter things in my life, and a little bit about Dr. Collins, my college applications, how much I want to get into Barnard, and a little bit about Annie and Bill and the party we're going to have next Saturday.

But a lot of time, we talked seriously about David and death and change. We did most of our talking Friday night. I asked him first if he'd noticed anything different in David before going away to school.

"Not particularly," Jimmy said. "I've tried to think about it, but I can't really remember him angrier or anything. When I think I can, I generally assume it's hindsight. He was angry. He was always angry."

"I know something was different," I said. "That

last day. There was some change in him, but I can't pin down just what it was."

"Maybe," Jimmy said. "But I can't help you with that."

"When you heard," I asked, "were you surprised?"

Jimmy looked thoughtful. "I really was," he said. "You weren't, were you?"

"Not very much," I said. "Not once I accepted it."

"Yeah," he said. "Of course, you knew David better than I did, and I've been away from home the past couple of years and hadn't seen as much of him. But I always assumed he'd outgrow his anger. He'd go away to college, and who knows, maybe he'd search out his natural parents and find them, and resolve that for himself. And then he'd come to peace with Bob and Lorraine. He might never be close to them, but you don't have to be close to your parents when you're an adult. It's nice if you are, but it isn't required."

"They were really horrible to him," I said. There was no one else I could say that to. "They never understood him."

"You know more about that than I do," Jimmy said. "I remember when David was a kid, the fights and everything, but I don't know how things were lately."

"You were here last summer."

"I wasn't paying much attention last summer," Jimmy said. "Last summer most of my attention was focused on me. Getting over Betty."

"You're better off without her."

"Probably," Jimmy said. "But I'm glad you didn't tell me that last summer."

I smiled. Last summer, Jimmy was sure his life was

at an end because Betty dumped him. I never much liked Betty anyway, but I had kept quiet about it.

"Things never got better between David and his parents?" Jimmy asked.

"He was home less," I said. "That probably helped things out a little. But they made such incredible demands on him. They insisted he run for junior class president, and when he lost, they cut off his allowance for a month because they didn't think he'd tried hard enough. And he really did try. He just wasn't as popular as Judd. But Bob and Lorraine just wouldn't believe that."

"But you don't know what made him finally . . ." Jimmy obviously couldn't get out the words.

"Not unless he told me that last day. I can't remember what we talked about that day."

"Except that you were bothered by it."

"I think," I said. "I'm pretty sure."

"How are you now?" he asked. "Really."

"Still shaken," I said.

"Are you sleeping better?" he asked, with a little grin.

"My urges to call you at three in the morning are a little weaker," I said. "I'm really sorry about all those calls."

"Don't be silly," Jimmy said. "It got my mind off school."

"I'm glad to have been of service," I said, and giggled.

Jimmy smiled, and then closed his eyes and rested his head against the back of the chair. "It's rough when somebody dies," he said. "When I was a sophomore, a kid I knew committed suicide. Do you remember anything about that?"

"I don't think so," I said.

"I didn't know him well," Jimmy said. "And it was just a suicide. No other deaths. But even so it shook me up for weeks. I never really believed in death before that. But all of a sudden Ted didn't exist. I was terrified. Even though I knew he did it to himself, he was the one who put the rope there and tied the noose and stuck his head through it. If he could die, anybody could. You, me, Mom, and Dad. Anybody. And I didn't much like that idea."

"But you got over it?"

"Yeah," he said, scratching his head thoughtfully. "And you will too. It's going to take you longer, because David did it with such a goddamn flourish, but you'll get over it. Recovery is one of the real joys of life."

"I hope you're right," I said.

"I hope so too," he said, with a smile. "And feel free to call me anytime you need to."

One thing I didn't do this weekend was read David's notebooks. I almost did Saturday night, but my stomach clenched up just thinking about it. I'm not sure why I'm so reluctant to, but I am. I know I have to finish reading them, but I also know I don't want to. As a matter of fact, I can think of about a thousand things I'd rather do than finish the notebooks. Like crossing the Atlantic in a life raft.

Maybe when I wake up tomorrow the notebooks will be gone. Maybe the notebooks fairy will have sneaked into my room and whisked them away (leaving a quarter under my pillow).

Maybe I'll wake up tomorrow and find myself adrift on a life raft in the middle of the Atlantic. Somehow that seems more likely these days.

November 30

No matter how hard I've tried, I haven't been able to finish the notebooks. And since I hate having them hang over me, I decided to tackle it head on with Dr. Collins. "I can't finish them," I said. "I don't have that much left, but I can't get myself to finish them."

"Why do you think that is?" Dr. Collins asked.

"You're not going to do that all session, are you?" I asked. "Answer me with questions. It drives me crazy."

"Would you prefer it if I just gave you advice?" he asked, half smiling.

"No, of course not," I said. "I wouldn't do it anyway."

"That's what I figured," he said. "So why do you think you can't finish the notebooks?"

"The pain is too great," I said. "I just can't."

"Okay," Dr. Collins said. "That makes sense."

"You lack conviction," I said.

"No, I believe you," he said. "I think there's more to it though."

"And I have to figure it all out," I said. "This is

just like school. I do all the work and you get paid for it."

Dr. Collins laughed. "I work too," he said.

"Yeah, I know," I said. "And your overhead in tissues must be incredible."

"It adds up," he said. "Do you think there are any other reasons why you can't finish the notebooks?"

I sighed.

"How do you feel when you read them?" he asked.

"Awful," I said.

"Is that all?" he asked, tilting his head toward me. "Don't you ever feel anything else besides awful?"

"What do you mean?" I asked.

"Are all the memories unpleasant ones?"

"Yes," I said, then "no. That's a lie. Sometimes they're funny. Sometimes David is. And it's funny seeing the world through his eyes. And sometimes they're just uncomfortable, when he's looking at me, or somebody I care about. And sometimes when he's saying something nice about me, or about my family, it feels good. I feel like he's smiling at me." I closed my eyes, and tried to picture David smiling, but the image was faint. David never did smile very much. He had a sardonic grin that he used a lot, but his smiles were special treats.

"And if you finish reading the notebooks, what will happen?" Dr. Collins asked.

"I'll lose David," I said. "That's what you mean, isn't it?"

"I think that's something you're afraid of, yes," he said.

"But I can't lose David," I said. "I never will. Not the good stuff. No matter how old I get, David's always going to be a part of me. I'm not worried about that."

"The thing about any close relationship," Dr. Collins began, and I could see he was being careful with his choice of words, "is that you go through certain experiences together. You share them. The experiences depend on what your relationship with the person is, but there are shared moments. When you lose someone through death or divorce or just distance, you no longer share those experiences. And there's loss there. There will be moments or days when you'll think to yourself, 'if only so and so were here to share this with me.'"

"I understand all that," I said.

"With the notebooks, you still have something to share with David," he said. "They're a fresh experience for you, and since they're in his voice, you're sharing it with him. He meant you to, after all. Pain and joy, all of it. It's there from him to you to share."

"And when I've finished, there won't be anything new for us to share," I said. "And I'll have to start dealing with life completely without David. Is that what you mean?"

"Yeah," he said. "That's basically what I mean."

I thought about that for a moment. "You may be right," I said finally. "That's probably part of it. Although David is so alive in me right now, I can't really think I'm worried about losing him."

"Do you think there are other reasons then?" Dr. Collins asked. "Why you can't finish reading the notebooks."

"No," I said. "That must be it."

"Now you lack conviction," he said. "Obviously there's more to it than that, Lynn. What is it?"

"Maybe there is," I said, almost defiantly. "Did it ever occur to you that the closer I get to the end of the notebooks, the closer I get to the end of David's life?"

"I thought that was what we were just talking about," Dr. Collins said.

"David didn't just die, you know," I said, feeling all my muscles clench up into one giant knot. "If he'd died in an accident or something, I don't think I'd be here right now. Jeffrey certainly wouldn't be crazy somewhere. A lot of things that happened wouldn't have happened. Too many to count."

"I don't get what you're saying," Dr. Collins said.

"I don't want to know why David killed his parents," I said, trying very hard not to cry. "Himself. I don't want to know. I don't want to see what made him do it. I don't want his version of his last few weeks, his last few days. For all I know, his last few minutes. There's only so much pain I can take. Do you blame me?"

"You don't know the notebooks go that far," he said.

"They must," I said, and took a deep breath. "Or fairly close to it. I've read three quarters of the last one, and it's practically June. You know, you say I want to go on sharing things with David, and maybe I do. Maybe you're right. When I see a good photograph, I think of him. Like a reflex. But that doesn't mean I want to share everything with him. When David was alive, I refused to share a lot of stuff with him. A lot of his pain. I took as much as I could, but I couldn't take it all. Nobody could have taken it all. Not even you."

Dr. Collins tilted his head, but he didn't say any-thing.

"I don't want to share their deaths," I said, and there I was, crying all over again. Dr. Collins slid the tissue box over to me. "If I don't finish the note-books, I don't have to take that chance."

"But what are the consequences of your not finish-ing them?" he asked. His voice was so soft, so gentle, I almost didn't hear him.

"I'll go crazy," I admitted. "Not Jeffrey-ranting crazy. But slowly crazy. Like when you're on a diet and all you can think about is food. All I'll think about is David. I'll never get him out of my system. I know that."

"So what do you think you should do?"

"How about a frontal lobotomy?" I asked, manag-ing a grin.

Dr. Collins smiled. "Short of that," he said.

"I'll read them," I said. "I don't think David left me much choice."

"No," Dr. Collins said. "I never met him, but it doesn't sound to me as if David liked giving people choices."

Part of me wanted to leap to David's defense. I still hate it when people put David down. But then I real-ized Dr. Collins was on my side. Really, totally, com-pletely on my side.

"I'll read it," I said, and swallowed hard. "I've gone this far with David. I might as well go all the way."

"Call me," Dr. Collins said. "I mean that, Lynn. If you can't handle it, if it's too rough for you to deal with alone, call me. If I'm not in, I'll leave word with my service to have your call placed through."

"Thank you," I said, feeling sort of honored. "But I'll be okay."

I just hope I wasn't lying about that one.

December 1

I went to the hospital this afternoon and visited Annie. She's still in the body cast, but she says it's going to come off in a couple of weeks, and they're talking about springing her by Christmas.

She seemed a lot better. I told her about Bill and the upcoming party. There was a lot of gossip to fill her in on. Somehow, while I wasn't watching, the class started coming back to life. Danny finally asked Tracy out (she's only wanted that since third grade), and Steffi and Charlie split up when she found out he was also dating a junior, and Tommy announced to everybody that he was gay, and then seemed annoyed when none of us were shocked. That kind of thing. Annie really enjoyed hearing it all, and it was fun for me to tell her.

It's a good sign that things are moving again. It's going to take me longer, I think, to get back to normal, but if the other kids can, I can too.

I feel like the only thing holding me back are the

notebooks. So I've firmly resolved to read them tomorrow night. I'm going to finish that chapter of my
life and David's, and then maybe I'll be normal again
too.

Bill's party Saturday night will be my reward and a
celebration. I'm due a fresh start, and I really want
one.

December 2

I am reeling. My stomach hurts again the way it did
when I first learned what David did. I don't feel like
crying, not yet, but I know I will, and I'm not sure
that when I start, I'll be able to stop. I know I'm going to have to tell my parents, but I can't, not yet.
Right now I can barely hold this pen, I'm shaking so
hard. I didn't think David held any more shocks for
me, but I underestimated him. Oh, how I underestimated his gift for horror.

I decided it would be better if I got the notebooks
out of the way a day before Bill's party so tonight I
gritted my teeth and took out that final notebook and
started reading. And it hurt. God, did it ever. It
wasn't even that what David was writing about was so
painful. For the most part it wasn't, although I think

he was getting angrier and angrier. But maybe I made that up 20/20 hindsight. It's just it was all so fresh, so vivid. I thought the other stuff was, but it was nothing compared to all this. He'd mention buying a book, and I could remember the exact day he bought it, and the discussion of whether he should keep it here, where his parents wouldn't find it, or whether he should brave their wrath, so he'd be able to read it that night. He'd mention a TV show, and I'd remember our discussing it the next day at school. I loved it; he thought it was junk. I didn't know anything so unimportant could be so painful.

I stopped near the very end, because I didn't think I could go on anymore. And then I remembered what Dr. Collins had said about holding onto David through the notebooks, and I decided to show him and finish the damn things. God, what an idiot I can be.

So I kept reading. It wasn't easy, because I started crying around then, and I got really nervous about smudging the pages with my tears. Somehow at the time, that seemed like a very important consideration.

The notebooks went on through the beginning of the summer. David spent July here with us, and he didn't write much. What he did write was about us, how much he enjoyed staying here. And I was remembering everything, every goddamn detail, and crying, and putting my stereo on louder and louder so Mom and Dad wouldn't hear me, not that my tears are anything new to them right now.

I got to the last page, and I couldn't read it. I just couldn't. I should have listened to my instincts and thrown the notebooks out then, unfinished, but idiot that I am images of Dr. Collins floated through my mind, and I picked up the notebook and read it all.

God, I'm shaking so hard now the house must be trembling.

The last couple of pages were about Bob and Lorraine's return, how upset David was to have to move back in with them. But he didn't sound angry, not the way he could be. It had been his choice, after all. No, it was more resignation. Sorrow. Pain. I think that hurt more to read than the anger would have.

Until the very last line. That last line. That goddamn death sentence.

All David wrote were three words. "Lorraine is pregnant."

God, what did David do?

Much, much later

Lorraine wanted to have a baby more than anything else in the world. I think I always knew that. Certainly by the time I became a teen-ager, I got offhanded confidences from her and secondhand ones from Mom. She and Bob went to see every fertility specialist in the area once every two years; they would start with one, and sweep through ten more until by the time they'd finished with the last one, it was time to start with the first one again. They kept hoping for miraculous new cures for whatever form of infertility was causing their problem. I remember one evening when we had them all over for dinner, and Bob discussed sperm counts over the chicken curry. I loved the image of them all counting.

Lorraine even had an operation at one point to try

and help, although it didn't seem to at the time.
David stayed here.

Mom and Dad wanted Bob and Lorraine to be able
to have a baby, of course, but they didn't like their
obsessiveness about it. Mom got very upset when she
came across Lorraine giving me a lecture on the
newest techniques for conception. Mom didn't think
it was an appropriate thing for a twelve year old to
be discussing. I, of course, was absolutely fascinated
and very angry at Mom for putting a stop to the conversation.

"There are some things Lorraine shouldn't be discussing with you," Mom told me after Lorraine left.
"Lorraine really can't help herself, because she wants
a baby so much, but it's not something she should be
talking about with you."

"Why not?" I asked, sure she was going to say I was
too young for that sort of topic.

"Because you're David's friend," Mom said instead.
"And you might tell him what Lorraine told you, and
it's all stuff he'd be better off not knowing."

"Why?" I asked again, but this time I was just curi-
ous.

"Think about how it must make David feel," Mom
said. "Knowing his parents want to have a baby so
much. Knowing he's adopted."

So I thought about it. "Awful," I finally said.

"Yeah," Mom said. "I think so too. Like he isn't
good enough for them; they aren't satisfied with
him."

"But they're not," I said. I may have only been
twelve, but I'd known that for years.

"Oh, Lynn," Mom said and sighed. "In their own
way Bob and Lorraine love David."

The funny thing was I knew she was wrong. I wasn't sure whether she believed what she had said, or whether she just thought all parents loved their children and therefore Bob and Lorraine must have loved David, or whether she was lying to me because I was David's friend, or because I was just twelve. But I knew she was wrong. David knew it too. And if he'd had any doubts, Bob and Lorraine's obsession with pregnancy must have made it clear to him.

"Why don't they just adopt another kid?" I asked Mom about two years ago. "If they're that determined, why not just try another adoption?"

"They want their own child," Mom said.

"You mean they think if they adopted again, they'd end up with another David," I said.

"That's got to be part of it," Mom said. "Anyway, it's hard to come by perfect white babies these days, and they wouldn't take anything else."

So Bob and Lorraine continued to make the rounds of specialists. I guess one of them must have finally worked. Because David couldn't have meant anything else by that final "Lorraine is pregnant."

The awful thing is that it all makes sense to me now. David must have been devastated to find out Lorraine was pregnant. God knows how he learned, but David was always finding things out. If nothing else, he eavesdropped.

God, poor David. Some part of him must have wanted his parents to love him, to accept him for who he was. And he had to know if they had a baby that was that. They'd never love him. I wasn't even that sure they'd want to see him again. They'd probably throw him out like a bad investment. And if I could picture Bob and Lorraine doing that to him, I can imagine what David was fantasizing.

Even his note makes sense now. He must have thought that if Bob and Lorraine had another child, they'd ruin that life as well. I don't know if he was right about that. Maybe if it were their own baby, they'd be able to love and accept it. But I wasn't David, and much as I knew about him and his parents, there had to be things even I didn't know. Maybe he was right. He was certainly entitled to his opinion.

But God, the way he chose to act on it. I've been trying for what seems like forever to come to grips with what David did, but now there's a whole new tragedy to deal with. Lorraine was pregnant and David knew it. He killed a pregnant woman. Two lives for the price of one. Did the police know?

I can't tell Mom and Dad. I just can't. I'm not sure if I'll ever tell anybody, but I can't tell them. Not now. I can't bear the idea of seeing their faces. Not now. I just can't.

There's something else. What if that's what David told me at lunch? What if that's what I can't hear him say? It certainly would have left me feeling disturbed. Maybe I just half heard him, or maybe I didn't believe him until it was too late. I don't feel like I knew it and had just forgotten, but maybe I've completely deceived myself. If David did tell me Lorraine was pregnant that day, shouldn't I have been able to stop him? I would have known he was disturbed. Could I have stopped him? Could I have guessed what he planned?

I don't need Dr. Collins to know I wasn't responsible for what David did. But I can't help being afraid maybe I could have changed things. If David had told me that day Lorraine was pregnant, I would have known enough to be concerned. To offer David a helping hand. Just to invite him over after school, maybe ask him to stay for supper. Change my plans with Steffi. Such minor things.

I hope that wasn't what David told me that day. Maybe we just talked about the weather or baseball or philosophy.

I close my eyes, but all I can picture is David sneering. And I can't be sure who he's sneering at.

December 4

DISASTER!

Yesterday was one of those days I'll dream about for the rest of my life, the kind my mother used to say someday I'd laugh at, when she and I both knew perfectly well I never would.

It started with my getting about three hours sleep all last night. I'd finally fall asleep, but then I would wake up with a start. I wasn't even dreaming about David. I don't remember dreaming about anything. I just remember waking up all shaky. Then it would take forever to fall back asleep.

Everything came flooding back to me. Everything

except what David said to me that last day. That one is still locked up. But everything else, every word, every nuance, every damn pause. I remembered it all.

I didn't get out of bed until eleven, even though I'd been awake for hours. And then I remembered Bill's party, and it was all I could do to keep from crawling back into bed.

Fresh start. Celebration. I wanted to throw up.

I thought about calling Bill up and saying I didn't feel well enough, that I had a cold, but I knew he was counting on me. And I didn't want to have to face my parents, who've been so excited about the party, and my going out, and becoming a normal American teen-ager again.

So I figured I'd better go; it just seemed easier than not going.

I went down eventually and nibbled on some toast. Mom asked me if I'd like to go shopping, get a new dress for the party, but that was practically the last thing I felt like doing. So I said something ridiculous about catching up with my homework and went back upstairs.

I thought I would cry then, but I didn't, not all day. I just ached and felt hollow, like my insides had just been blown out of my body, and I was just left empty. I could almost hear the echo when my heart beat.

I don't know how long I was upstairs, but at some point, when I really wasn't ready for it, the phone rang. It was Bill, saying that his cousin who lives in the city would be able to come to the party after all. Bill had been hoping he would, and I was happy for him (as happy as I could be, in the depths of my misery). So I congratulated him, and agreed, once again, to come a half hour earlier than everybody else, and approve all the arrangements. Earn my co-host status.

I tried to do some homework after that, to get my mind off David, but I couldn't concentrate. Mom even came upstairs at one point to see if I was okay, but I told her (through the closed door) that I was just fine. We both knew I was lying, but there was no point pressing it, so she went away. I could hear her and Dad talking though, those hushed, concerned tones that meant they knew something was the matter and they weren't quite sure what to do about it.

Did Bob and Lorraine ever talk like that about David?

When I couldn't postpone it any longer, I went to the bathroom, took a shower, dressed for the party, in my blue and white dress, and went downstairs. Mom and Dad went on and on about how good I looked. They must have been lying. Inside, I was aching as bad as I ever have, and there's no way that didn't show. Anyway, Dad drove me to the party, and when he started to ask me if I was okay, he withdrew the question, as though he knew he'd be better off if he didn't hear the answer.

I was very precariously balanced. I didn't want to mess things up for Bill, but all I wanted to be was home alone.

And then I started thinking about how I wanted to be back at David's, in his room, surrounded by him. It was the strangest feeling. It was like if I were there, I could get all the grief and anger out of my system. I know it was irrational. The pain I felt obviously wasn't going to go away in one marathon session, but knowing that didn't help. I wanted to be there, and

having to go to Bill's, to a party at that, made me
overwhelmingly resentful. I really hated Bill for having that party, which is a hell of a fine attitude for
a cohost to have.

Dad let me out at the door, watched to make sure
somebody let me in, then drove off. I wanted to run
after him, get into the car, and demand to be driven
back to David's. God, I wanted that.

"Hi, Bill," I said, trying to smile.

"You look awful," he said. "Do you feel all right?"

So instead of telling him the truth, that I didn't
feel well, and would probably have a terrible time at
the party and ought to go home immediately, I put
on the falsest smile in the history of hypocrisy, and
said I felt just fine and was really looking forward to
meeting his cousin.

So we went in, and I put my coat on the bed in
Bill's room upstairs. I really didn't think I'd be able
to get through the evening at that point, but I felt
that since I was there, I was committed and might as
well try not to depress everybody else. So I plastered
that smile on my face again and went downstairs to
the family room.

It really looked good, festive but casual. Mr. and
Mrs. Newman were there with Bill's cousin, Mike. I
said hello to all of them and tried to make small talk.

Fortunately, the first few kids were early, and the
party got started. Mr. and Mrs. Newman went upstairs, the stereo got turned on, people were dancing
and talking and eating, and the party seemed to be
quite a success.

Bill asked me to dance a couple of times; the first
time I refused, but the second time I accepted. It was

a slow number, and I just held onto him, hardly moving my body.

It was the strangest sensation. I was there, at the party, but I wasn't a part of it. I observed everything, who was flirting with who, who was hurt she hadn't been asked to dance, who was scared to ask who, all of it, but I observed myself just as sharply. It was like we were all on TV and I was watching it in complete privacy. And the funny thing is that it wasn't unpleasant. I liked the feeling of knowing more about what was going on than anybody else. There was a comfort to detachment. Even when I was clinging to Bill, I was as aware of the effect we were making as of the sensation of holding onto him, just barely swaying to the music.

Naturally, I didn't socialize much during the party. I was asked to dance some more, but I said I had a headache and didn't really feel like it. Instead, I watched and listened in on conversations. My behavior's been so weird lately that everyone's used to my eccentricities by now, and nobody made a fuss or tried to force me to be more active.

The couple of times I lost my detachment, I thought about David, and the parties we'd been at together. But when I thought about that, my head would just start spinning, and I had to make an effort to regain my detachment. I closed my eyes and counted to a hundred until I was all right again.

Bill's cousin Mike was being very social, without any help from me. I noticed he was talking to a group of kids, Steffi included, but I really wasn't listening to what they were saying. I was working best on an impressions level; specifics bogged me down. But at one of those moments when everything is silent (the records were being flipped over, conversation had suddenly lulled), I heard him say, "You know, it's like that old joke, where the kid who murders his parents throws himself on the mercy of the court because he's an orphan."

There was a sharp intaking of breaths; we did it as one.

"Well," Steffi said. "I wonder if that would have been David's defense."

A couple of kids tittered. I gasped.

Mike said, "What?"

"Steffi, that was uncalled for," I said. I wasn't even sitting near her. I said it across the playroom.

I have a theory now that it's the next day, and I've regained some objectivity. I think Steffi made that stupid awful remark to help out poor Mike from his stupid awful remark. Of course his was made in ignorance, but if hers were made as some sort of charitable gesture, it does excuse it slightly. Last night, however, I had no theories, just a raw horror.

"Oh, no," Steffi said. "Not another little talk from Lynn. All about poor David and how we must never forget."

I sat there, my mouth open.

Steffi used my silence as a chance to attack some more. "If Lynn had raised funds for David's defense fund, he'd have been out on bail in ten minutes flat," she said. "Unless of course she'd had to go into the cafeteria to get the money. Lynn's the only person I've ever known who's scared to go into a school cafeteria. It reminds her too much of her precious David."

"Stop it, Steffi," Judd said.

"I will not," she said. "I've been putting up with

this nonsense for months now. David this and David that. Lynn's forgotten that the living have feelings too. Feelings and rights. Like the right not to be reminded all the time of what some poor sick boy did."

"It's only been three months," I said. "Less."

"I'm sure you know to the minute how long it's been," she said. "You probably have to stop watch to make sure we all grieve the appropriate amount of time. I'm surprised you didn't have us all dress in black for this party. More of a wake atmosphere."

Someone said, "Steffi."

"I'm just sick of it all," she said. "The way Lynn goes on, like she had a monopoly on suffering. The way she's holding onto her pain. Maybe she thinks if she grieves more it means David loved her more. Of course, Jeffrey outdid her, but she seems to have forgotten about that."

"Steffi, that's enough," Judd said. "Now, just cut it out, okay?"

"I will not," she said. She looked so cold, so mean. "She has you all feeling so sorry for her, especially now, when all I'm doing is telling the truth. Telling the same truth that we've all discussed. How ridiculous Lynn's being. How melodramatic. I just think it's about time she heard it. Maybe if she sees what we all think of her, she'll come to her senses and stop acting like she's David's widow or something."

Yet another mistake coming up. If I'd had half a brain, I would have just kept my mouth shut and started crying. God knows, all I wanted to do all day was cry, and I was finally handed the excuse. But no. Schmuck that I am, I had to open my big mouth.

"You're just jealous, that's all," I said. No, to be honest about it, I shrieked. I never knew my voice could reach that level of shriek. "You wanted to screw David since the day you first saw him, and he never gave a damn about you. You chased after him all last year, you made a goddamn idiot of yourself over the prom. You even came onto Jeffrey, hoping that David would get jealous. Half the reason David shot himself was to escape from you."

Steffi gasped, like I'd struck her, and then she started to cry. She always did cry easily. She cries like she's on a TV show, tiny well-formed tears. No runny nose for Steffi. Just genteel little sobs. She can go to hell.

A few of the kids went over to her to comfort her. Nobody came near me, and I don't blame them. I was ready to take a swing at anybody, until the detached part of me took control again. Then I just watched and grinned. Because, in a ghoulish way, it was kind of funny.

"Do you feel all right?" Tracy asked me.

"No," I said. "I'm going to go home."

"That's all right," Steffi sniffed from her corner. "I'll leave."

"Don't be ridiculous," Bill said. I'm not sure which one of us he said it to.

"I have a headache," I said, then started laughing. It was such a time-honored excuse, and so meaningless. I didn't have a headache just then. My entire being, soul and body, ached beyond belief. My head felt clear and healthy. "I'll walk home."

"I'll drive you," Bill said curtly. So we went upstairs and got our coats. He got the keys to his parents' car and we got in.

We drove home in silence, but when he parked for

me to get out he said softly, "You can't let this thing about David eat away at you."

"I'm not," I said.

"You are," he said. "I know what obsession looks like. Let it be. David's dead and you're alive and you have to live with that."

"You don't believe what Steffi said about me, do you?" I asked. Things were bad enough without Bill believing all that garbage.

"No more than I believe what you said about her," he said. "I do believe you're desperately unhappy, and you need help."

"I'm seeing a shrink," I said sharply. "What more do you want from me?"

"I don't want anything," he said, and stroked my arm gently. "Except for you to be happy."

One final mistake for the road. Did I tell Bill the truth, that I'd been shaky all day? Did I offer him a reasonable explanation for my unreasonable behavior? Certainly not.

"You don't understand," I said coldly. "You can't possibly understand. You didn't know David. You don't know what he was like, how close we were. Don't presume that you do."

"I wouldn't dream of presuming," he said, and reached past me to open my door. So I got out and went back to my house, where I had to explain, in as few words as possible, why I was coming home at 10:30 from a party I'd helped arrange and had genuinely looked forward to.

December 5

Steffi and I were very cool to each other today. I gave
a little thought to apologizing to her, but I couldn't.

Damn it, she started it. And she *was* chasing after
David.

I wonder how much Dr. Collins is going to know
before he even sees me.

December 6

I visited Annie in the hospital this afternoon. I guess
I thought she wouldn't have heard anything about
the party, but of course she had.

"You can't hold onto anger," she told me.

"I've only been angry at Steffi since Saturday," I said.

"That's not true," she said. "You've been angry at her a lot longer than that."

"Since she spoke to the reporter, then," I said. "But I wasn't really mad about that. Not any longer. I've only been really mad since Saturday."

"Then you're angry at something else," she said. "Because I know what anger looks like, and you've been angry every time I've seen you since David died."

She and Bill would make a great pair. He recognizes obsession, she recognizes anger. Between the two of them, they could set up a business recognizing negative emotions.

There's probably a lot of money in that.

December 7

Dr. Collins had the nerve to pretend he didn't know anything about the party. Professional ignorance, or something like that.

So I told him about it, a little more viciously than I might otherwise have. It's a shame Annie didn't see me then; my anger was very easily recognizable. Even Dr. Collins spotted it.

"When somebody a person loves dies, the survivors frequently feel anger," he said, oh so casually. "Especially in the case of a suicide. The survivors feel the person who has committed suicide has cheated them somehow, treated them badly by taking his own life. And, of course, the anger intermingles with guilt. The survivors feel guilty that they are angry and will deny to themselves that they feel resentful toward the person who died."

"I admit, I'm angry," I said. "I'm angry at Steffi and I'm angry at Bill and I'm angry at Annie and I'm angry at you. With all that anger, I don't have time to be angry at David also."

"Anger makes its own time," he said.

"Are you saying I'm angry at David?"

"I'm not saying anything," he said. "But that's not an uncommon reaction to a suicide."

"I'm not angry at David," I said. "I think right now he's the only one I'm not angry at."

"But if he hadn't committed suicide, you wouldn't have been angry at all those other people," Dr. Collins said. "You wouldn't even know me to be angry at me."

"If my parents hadn't conceived me, I wouldn't know any of these people to be angry at," I said. "But that doesn't make me angry at my parents."

Neither one of us was particularly satisfied with my answer. But I don't feel satisfied with anything, so why should therapy be any different?

Things in school are awful. It's like Steffi and I have surrounded ourselves with armed camps—some kids definitely siding with her, others with me (not that

I particularly want them to). And then there are a few go-betweens like Tracy and Judd, who are trying to stay friends with both of us.

I wonder if they're getting headaches from this situation too.

In addition to all that, I've been feeling really terrible about Bill, and how I messed up his party. It astounds me he's still talking to me.

December 8

After school today, I went to Bill and asked him if we could talk.

"All right," he said. "Maybe we should."

So we went over to Juniors. Steffi was there, with her little coterie, and I thought about asking Bill if we could go somewhere else. But then I decided dammit, she didn't own the place, and we went in. She left about two minutes later, so I guess I won that round.

"I want to apologize," I said. "For the party and how I behaved and for the way I acted afterward when you took me home."

"It's okay," Bill said.

"No, it isn't," I said. "It really isn't. But there are

some things that happened . . ." I realized I didn't want to tell Bill about the notebooks. And then I realized I hadn't told anybody about finding them yet, not my parents, not Lieutenant Donovan. I hadn't even told Dr. Collins about the last entry. I don't know why. I certainly know it's something I have to do.

"Lynn," Bill said. "Where are you?"

"What?" I said.

"You know, I don't think there's ever been a time when the two of us have been alone together when you've been a hundred percent there," Bill said. "Am I that boring?"

"Oh Bill," I said. "Don't make me feel worse. I'm trying to apologize as it is."

"I'm sorry," he said and then he smiled. "I was just teasing."

"I wish you'd known me last year," I said. "Last year I was so different . . ."

Bill made comforting noises after that, and I guess we talked for a while longer. But I wasn't a hundred percent there. I wasn't even fifty. Because for the first time I realized just how angry I was at David.

It was bad enough what he did. Did he have to leave it to me to clean up the mess he left behind?

December 9

I told Dr. Collins I'd finished the notebooks.

It felt good discussing with him what my alternatives were. It wasn't that he said very much, but he listened and just talking out the problem helped. And I wasn't ready to talk about just how much I hated David right then.

I want to destroy the notebooks, but I don't know whether I ought to. David left them for me, and I assume he thought I would do the right thing with them, but that doesn't mean he didn't think they should be destroyed. He might have wanted to, but had not had the opportunity. Still, he might have wanted me to keep them, to remember him by, or as a testament to what he was, to his existence. Or maybe I should give them to Donovan. Or even to the Squabblers.

We finally decided that it was silly of me to try to make the decision on my own. That's what parents are for, to help out. So tomorrow, when Mom gets back from the gallery, I'll talk to her and Dad about it.

December 10

After supper I told Mom and Dad there was something I wanted to talk to them about. I admit I felt amused by their concerned looks. There were so many awful things I could be getting ready to tell them.

"I found David's notebooks," I said instead. "We had them hidden in our attic."

"I'm not surprised," Mom said. "When?"

"A while ago," I said. "I finished reading them last Saturday."

"No wonder you were so upset," she said. "Were they very bad?"

"They were hard going," I said. "He hurt so much. But he loved us all a great deal."

"I'm glad for that," she said. "At least he knew someone loved him."

"He knew," I said.

"Do you want to tell us about what was in them?" Mom asked.

"No," I said, shaking my head. "Not yet. Okay?" Mom nodded.

"What are you going to do with them?" Dad asked.

"I don't know yet," I said. "That's what I wanted to discuss with you. I don't even know if they're legally mine."

"For all practical purposes, they are," Dad said. "He left them to you, and he kept them here. Besides, I doubt even the Squabblers would think David's journals are worth a court case."

"Part of me wants to destroy them," I said. "They're really awful to read."

"Do you think you should?" Mom asked.

"I don't know," I said. "It's eerie having them around. I've only read them once, and I don't have any desire to go back and reread any of them, but they're still overwhelming me. If I do keep them, I'd prefer not to have them around."

"We could keep them locked in our safe," Dad said. "Then you'd know where they were if you ever did want to read them again, but you wouldn't be confronted with their existence all the time."

I thought about that. "That sounds pretty good," I said. "I want them put away somewhere where I don't have to think about them."

"All right," Dad said. "We'll keep them there, until you decide you want to have them or destroy them."

"There's something else," I said. "Lieutenant Donovan might be interested in seeing them."

"Oh, that's right," Dad said. "Do you want to show them to him?"

"I think so," I said, angry at David still and guilty at my anger. "They're my notebooks. I can bring them to him after school Monday." Maybe just getting them out of the house will help me get the distance I need right now from David, and the whole damn mess.

December 12

After school today, I went home, got the notebooks, and then biked over to the police station.

I'd been there before, on a class trip when I was in second grade (David, I remembered as soon as I saw the door, had thrown a tantrum and refused to go in), but I felt like a criminal anyway. Still, I found a clerk and asked where I could find Lieutenant Donovan. I was directed to a small office, and after he said I should enter, I did.

"I found the notebooks," I said, after I sat down. "And I thought you might like to see them."

He looked at me very thoughtfully. "Thank you," he said. "I would like to read them."

"I'd like them back," I said. "And I don't want just anybody reading them. They're his very private thoughts; they weren't intended for other people. Not even me, really."

"I'll be the only one to read them," he said. "I promise you that. And I'll make sure you get them back before the holidays."

"Thank you," I said and got up. I handed him

over the envelope with the notebooks in it. "My name and address is on the envelope, and inside too."

"I'll be careful with them," he said. "I must say I'm a bit surprised you brought them to me."

"I almost didn't," I said. "But you said if you understood David, maybe you could prevent other kids from doing what he did."

"That's my hope," he said. He didn't seem nearly as awful as I remembered.

"I don't know if they'll help," I said. "You'll understand David a lot better from reading them. I did, and I knew him very well. But whether you'll be able to use what you learned from him with somebody else, I don't know."

"But you brought them to me anyway."

"There are things in there I think you ought to know," I said. That was the most I could say. Let Donovan discover what for himself.

"Thank you," he said. "How's it been going?"

"Rough at first," I said. "Better now."

"Did you ever remember what the two of you talked about?" he asked.

I shook my head. "Not yet," I said. "Sometimes I think I never will, and sometimes I think I'm just about to. If it's important, I'll let you know."

"I'd appreciate that," he said. "Good-bye, Lynn."

"Good-bye," I said, and left the police station. I got on my bike and was fine until I got home. And then as soon as I put the bike back in the garage, I started shaking. My whole body just shook and shook, and I couldn't stop.

The awful thing is—I was shaking from a sense of relief.

December 13

I feel good.

I can't remember the last time I felt so good. Nothing bothers me, not even Steffi and the wall between us.

I smiled so much today my jaws hurt. And I laughed out loud at least ten times.

I even have this feeling that when the time is right, I'll remember what David told me that last day. And that it's foolish for me to try to remember until then.

If I'd known getting rid of the notebooks (even just temporarily) would make me feel so much better, I would have done it a long time ago.

December 14

I told Dr. Collins how good I felt, and he looked at me a little funny.

I guess if all his patients felt this good, he'd be out of business.

December 15

I got a call today from someone at Barnard asking if I was free to come into the city for an interview on Saturday.

"You'd better believe it!" I sang into the telephone. Barnard is my first choice college, after all.

The appointment is for eleven. Afterward, I'll have

lunch somewhere, and see if I can get a ticket for a matinee.

Oh, I hope the interview goes well!

December 17

I woke up feeling excited, dressed in just the right going-for-an-interview outfit (my green skirt and blouse, and my beige blazer. Very collegiate), received several dozen good wishes from Mom and Dad, got a lift to the train station, bought my ticket, kissed Dad goodbye (Mom's at the gallery on Saturdays until Christmas), got on the train, sat down, and got the shakes.

Oh, did I ever get the shakes. I could hardly hand the conductor my ticket to punch, I was shaking so hard.

I tried to tell myself it was just preinterview jitters. I took deep breaths. I took out the book I had in my pocketbook (a nice thick biography of Mary Queen of Scots, which I've read about half of. Carried, partly in case I did have time to read, and partly so that if the contents of my pocketbook should happen to fall all over the floor during the interview, they'd see I read high-class intellectual stuff), and tried to concentrate on that, but couldn't (I could scarcely hold the damn thing). I tried to picture myself in a relaxing setting, but the only thing I could see when I closed my eyes was blackness.

I got off to change trains at Jamaica, and for a moment, I thought about grabbing a train back home and admitting defeat, but I couldn't bear the thought of facing Mom and Dad. It was easier just to go ahead, and hope I calmed down before I got to Barnard. So I got onto the train going to Manhattan and decided to come to grips with my fear, by figuring out what was causing it.

That was no trick. It was going to New York that scared me so.

All right, I said to myself. What is it about New York?

That took a little longer to figure out. I pictured myself in New York, and I didn't seem scared. It was the train ride I was nervous about, not some fantasy version of running around the city and having a good time.

So I tried to figure out why I would be scared on a train going into New York, and then I realized I wasn't scared, not really. Not like I thought the train was going to crash. This was more like my feelings toward the cafeteria (lessened lately, although I still don't have lunch there if I have a choice, and I almost always have a choice).

And of course my cafeteria feelings are because of David.

So as soon as I thought of David, the fear started mingling with relief. Of course I was nervous because of David. That was natural enough once I thought about it. I always went into New York with David.

Last year we must have gone in a dozen times together, to see plays or movies or go to museums or
concerts. David and I always went to New York together. Somehow it was a comfort to both Mom and
Lorraine that we were together (each to protect the
other from muggers and rapists. And murderers).

Even when I was little, I went into New York with
David. Mom and Lorraine would take turns chap-
eroning us and Jimmy, when we'd go to the Statue
of Liberty or the Planetarium. Or sometimes all
five of us would go in together. But it was always
David and me. Riding on the train together. Excited
about what we'd be doing when we finally arrived.

I haven't been to New York since David died.

And that's why I was shaking and sweating and
palpitating.

Knowing why really helped, and by the time the
train went into the tunnel to Penn Station, I felt better. Not as eager as I had been when I got up this
morning, but under control and proud of myself for
doing it on my own. No parents, no Dr. Collins to
help me work things out. I was alone, and I managed
all right.

I took a cab from Penn Station to Barnard (which
cost a fortune), and after a few frantic minutes of
searching for the right building, located it, went in,
found the right room, and entered that. Somebody
was already in with Ms. Bullock, so I sat down,
straightened myself up, and looked around. I
breathed deeply then too, and I could feel the difference. This time it relaxed me.

By the time Ms. Bullock called me into her office, I
was feeling fine. I sat down, smiled at her, and behaved like a normal person. We exchanged some

standard small talk, then talked a little about what my plans were, why I was interested in Barnard, what activities I enjoyed most. I answered clearly and succinctly, and enjoyed hearing my voice. I was really quite articulate, and I could tell I was making a good impression. I tried hard to remember every question she was asking, so I could give Mom and Dad a full report when I got home (although I'd already decided to leave out the part about the train ride).

As a matter of fact, by that point, I was feeling so satisfied with myself, I almost wasn't paying attention to what Ms. Bullock was saying. But something in her tone caught me, and I listened when she said, "I meet an awful lot of girls doing this job."

"Um," I said, to show I was listening.

"A lot of the girls have been quite remarkable," she said. "People I've felt privileged to know, even for only a few minutes. But a lot of exceptional people are never discovered. They aren't flamboyant enough, or they keep so much under the surface."

"Like icebergs," I said.

"Exactly," she said. "And if you only ask standard questions, there's a real risk you'll only get standard answers. So occasionally, I ask an exceptional question. Just to see what kind of response I get." She smiled, to encourage me.

"All right," I said. "I guess I'm ready."

"Tell me," she said. "What do you think was the most significant event in your life?"

"What?" I said. Frankly, I thought her exceptional question would be about any contact I might have had with UFOs, or maybe something to do with previous incarnations. Nothing as mundane as significant events.

"A lot of girls say nothing significant has ever happened to them," she went on. "But then they think about it, and sure enough, something comes to mind. It might seem quite minor to somebody else, but to them it has great meaning. I find I learn a lot about girls that way."

"Significant event," I said, and then I started laughing.

"Do you find that funny?" she asked.

"I'm sorry," I said, trying to stop laughing. "Really. It's just this whole year has been so full of them, it's hard to know where to begin."

"Really," she said. "That sounds quite interesting. Please go on."

Where was I supposed to go? Especially as I was still trying to swallow a fatal attack of giggles. I thought briefly of lying (Well, during the last year this small country in the south of Europe offered me their crown, if only I would come and solve their various political and diplomatic crisis but the coronation date coincided with my SAT's . . .), but there was no lie that I could think of that would be safe or reasonable. So, trying very hard not to laugh anymore, I said, "A friend of mine died this past September."

"Oh," Ms. Bullock said. "I'm sorry to hear that."

"There have been . . . ramifications," I said, and I was so impressed with coming up with such a five-buck word that I immediately burst into roars of laughter. Real belly busters. Poor Ms. Bullock stared at me in horror.

"Please forgive me," I choked out. "I don't usually get hysterical."

"Can I get you something?" she asked. "A drink of water?"

At that point, I was so red in the face all I could do was wave my hands around. She took that to mean I wanted water, and ran out to get me some.

While she was gone, I deliberately put one foot on top of the other and stepped down as hard as I could. It hurt like hell, and the pain calmed me down, as I hoped it would. By the time Ms. Bullock came back in, I was practically human again. I took a couple of sips of water and apologized again.

"Forgive me," she said. "I never would have asked the question if I'd known it would be that upsetting to you."

So I told her a little bit about David and Jeffrey. Just bare skeletons, but enough for her to understand.

"I meet a lot of girls doing this job," she said again. "And I examine applications for a lot more girls I never have the chance to meet. And when I do it, I do it as a professional. Get to know what I need to know. Hear what I need to hear. Ask what I need answers to. It's a rare girl I remember six months after meeting."

I had the horrible feeling I would be one of the rare memorable ones.

"You forget," she said. "Or at least I forget that each of these girls has a life far beyond this interview. They've experienced pains and pleasures I couldn't even imagine. I shouldn't even try to. A girl once came in here two days after her father died. The funeral had been the day before, and here she was. She explained to me that her father would have wanted her to be there, that it had been his dearest hope that she would be able to attend Barnard. And then she started crying. She sat here for twenty minutes crying. There was nothing I could do."

"What an odd job," I said.

"Yes, it is," she said. "It really is. I never think about it that way, but you're absolutely right. It's an odd job."

"I've been shaky since it happened," I said. "But I'm getting better, believe it or not. I'm sure I'll be fine by next September."

She smiled at me. "I'm sure you'll be fine well before then," she said. "Don't worry. I asked you a very foolish question, and you responded by laughing. That's all there is to it."

"Thank you," I said.

"Thank you," she said. "And hang in there."

Mom and Dad got a judiciously censored account of all this at supper tonight. But I'm sure if Barnard turns me down, it won't be because of the interview. And that's something.

December 19

Annie was released from the hospital on Thursday, so I figured I'd visit her at home. I haven't seen her since right after the party, but we've spoken on the phone a couple of times.

Her mother told me she was upstairs in bed, and I went right up. What her mother didn't tell me was that Steffi was already there, chatting merrily with Annie as I walked in.

"Oh," I said.

"That's all right," Steffi said. "I was just leaving."

Annie looked like she'd like to get up and slug both of us.

"This is ridiculous," I said.

"I'm sorry," Steffi said coldly. "I said I'd leave."

"No, wait a second," I said. "I'm being ridiculous. Look, I lost my oldest friend this year. I don't want to lose my best friend as well."

Steffi stared at me. Annie showed me a pair of crossed fingers.

"Steffi, please," I said. "Do we have to keep acting like we hate each other? I don't hate you. I never did, except maybe for an awful moment at that party.

Won't you forgive me for the way I've been behaving."

"Even the interview?" she asked.

"Even the interview," I said. "You were handling things one way. I was handling them another. That doesn't mean either one of us was wrong."

She looked at me very carefully.

"Look," I said. This was my last shot. If she didn't go for this, I was going to throw the entire friendship out the window. "You're the one who's always after me to eat in the cafeteria. And I can't, if you're there and we're not speaking."

I thought I saw the beginnings of a smile.

"Please," I said. "For the sake of mental health, how about a little forgiveness?"

And she did smile. "You idiot," she said fondly, and we hugged each other. "I've hated hating you."

"It wasn't much fun, was it," I said. "Thank God, that's over."

"Sit down," Annie said. "Both of you. Steffi just got here, and I'm dying to hear everything."

"Hear everything?" Steffi said. "You've just been a witness to one of the major events of this school year."

"They'll be begging you for details," I said.

And we all laughed.

It felt real good.

December 20

I went to the police station after school today to pick up David's notebooks. Lieutenant Donovan was waiting with them for me.

"That poor kid," he said after we'd exchanged hellos. "He felt everything, didn't he? He had no protective shield."

"I guess not," I said. That hadn't been the reaction I'd expected from him, maybe because that hadn't been my reaction.

"We all live in private little hells," he said. "Even the happiest of us. There are always things that pain us. But to exist, you learn to live with the pain. You learn to protect yourself. I guess David never learned."

"He never gave himself the chance," I said.

"I don't think he could," Donovan said. "I don't want to speculate about him with you, since I know you cared very much about him, but judging from his notebooks, suicide was inevitable. The rest, though . . . Didn't his parents ever think about therapy for him? They must have sensed something was wrong."

"They didn't want to know," I said. "They were very good at shutting out reality."

"There's one more thing," Donovan said, and he looked very ill at ease.

I didn't know what he was going to say, but I knew I didn't want to hear it. "Yeah?" I said.

"David's mother wasn't pregnant," he said.

"But . . ."

"He must have been wrong," Donovan said. "Maybe he overheard her say she thought she was. Maybe he just thought she was. They'd tried to have a kid of their own, hadn't they?"

"Always," I said.

"That can make a kid a little hyper on the subject," Donovan said. "I don't know where David thought he got his information from, but we did an autopsy and Mrs. Morris was not pregnant at the time of her death."

"But that's why . . ." I began. "But . . . oh, my God!"

"I know, Lynn," Donovan said.

"But what David did," I cried. "It was . . . he was . . . dear God, it was crazy!"

"Oh, Lynn," Donovan said, and even I could see the pain in his eyes was for me. "Oh Lynn, of course it was."

December 22

This is all very weird. I'm writing it down as carefully as possible so that I can tell it to Dr. Collins accurately tomorrow.

It started last night when I had another dream about David. I've been dreaming less and less about him, and this was the first time in a week that I can remember that he showed up. I guess it's because of what Lieutenant Donovan told me.

Anyway, I had this dream about David. We were at school together, walking through the corridors, and it all seemed perfectly normal, until I realized we'd been walking and walking and not going anywhere. I asked nervously whether we should be in a class, but David said it was all right, it was lunch period, and I felt a little better.

So we went into the cafeteria, and suddenly David was wearing his famous blue outfit. The cafeteria was completely empty, and I thought, oh good, now I'll be able to hear what he's going to tell me. We sat down at our usual table, and David started talking to me. Only it was obvious he was just mouthing words. At first he was subtle about it, and I thought I really couldn't hear him, but then he became more and more grotesque about it, and I realized he didn't want me to hear him.

After a few moments of watching his mouth twist and turn, I lost all patience and shouted, "Stop it! If you want to tell me something, just say it."

David just smiled at me. He took his belt off, the one I'd given him, tied it into a noose, and stuck his head in it. And as he notched it tighter and tighter, he grinned at me.

I woke up shaken, and it was all I could do not to call Jimmy on the spot. It was like the past couple of months hadn't happened. But they had, and instead of calling, I got up, went to the bathroom, then went back to bed, and after a little while, fell back to sleep.

I was quiet at breakfast this morning, but at this point Mom and Dad are so used to my mood swings, they didn't seem to notice it. I went to school and managed to concentrate on the English test we had (although I flubbed my translations in Latin).

At lunch, Steffi joined me, and we began walking toward the cafeteria. It's one of those things, but yesterday, we hadn't had lunch there. I'd already made plans to have lunch with Judd and Tracy and Bill at Juniors, so today was my triumphant return day. The last place I felt like returning triumphantly to that day was the cafeteria, but with Steffi escorting me, I had to go in. I tried to hide my anxiety and chattered away about the English test (which was what everybody else was talking about anyway).

We walked in, and after getting our trays of food, we sat at our old table. I sat down, tried to concentrate on the conversation, and closed my eyes. And while they were closed, I could see David. He was smiling at me, but there was nothing horrible about it this time. It was just a smile. David didn't smile that way often, but it wasn't unfamiliar to me.

I thought, "David, tell me," and I could hear him saying back to me, "I don't have to. You know."

And I opened my eyes and I did know.

It was an overwhelming sensation. First, I felt like all the air had been squeezed out of my body, and then slowly, every part of me started to tingle. And then I felt so alive. I saw colors so much brighter than I'd ever seen them, and faces were fuller and more beautiful than I'd remembered.

"Excuse me," I said, wondering if I could ever express my love to them adequately. "I really feel very good right now, please don't worry, but I have to be alone for a few minutes."

"Are you sure you're all right?" Bill asked.

"Positive," I said. "I'll be back before lunch ends. Please, excuse me," and I got up and left the cafeteria.

It took me a moment to figure out where I could be alone, and then I remembered the auditorium. Sure enough it was empty, so I went in, sat close to the back, and remembered that last lunch.

We'd started by talking about Mr. Glick and what an idiot he was. Normal school talk. Normal David and Lynn talk. I think I mentioned Jimmy to him next, and we spent a little while running Betty down. All very normal.

I asked him then what he was giving his mother for her birthday, and he looked at me and gave me that rare smile and said, "I can't tell you. It's a surprise."

"Oh, come on, David," I said. "I won't tell her."

"No," he said. "This is one thing I can't tell you."
And he smiled again.

We went on from there to talk about what must
have been safer topics for him, movies, school gossip,
that kind of thing. But I was annoyed that he
wouldn't tell me what he'd gotten for Lorraine. I'd
kept a lot of David's secrets over the years, and I
didn't like the thought he didn't trust me with what I
assumed was a minor one.

But what had disturbed me, that little itching
feeling, was his smile. It was the way David looked
those rare moments when he was at peace with
himself. I couldn't think what there could be about
Lorraine's present that would give David peace.
Birthdays were always difficult for David because he
was adopted—one of those things that Bob and Lorraine had steadfastly refused to acknowledge. But this
year he wasn't miserable. And that wasn't right. That
was what bothered me.

It was such a small thing. No matter how I might
accuse myself, there was no way I could know what
David intended to do to Bob and Lorraine and himself because of one small secret and one small smile.
But he'd known. He'd planned, and the knowledge
that all their lives were about to end gave him a sense
of contentment.

I even think he deliberately did it two days before
Lorraine's birthday as kind of a present. She was
vain about her age; by killing her when he did, he
erased a full year from her obituaries.

Even though I felt better than I had in such a long
time, more at peace with myself than I could remember, I began to weep. Not just pretty little tears, but
real, from-the-gut sobbing. For Bob and Lorraine,

and for David, who lived in a world of such misery that the only way he could be happy was by destroying it all, and himself with it.

I don't know how long I sat there before Bill came in. He sat down next to me, then put his arm around my shoulder. He didn't say anything, but just sat there and held me as I cried. And maybe because he was there, I felt better sooner. I was filled with pity for them all, poor foolish Bob and poor foolish Lorraine and poor foolish David. What a mess they'd all made of their lives.

"Do you feel all right?" Bill asked me as I slowly stopped shuddering.

I managed to smile. "Would you believe me if I said yes?" I asked him.

He smiled back. "I just might," he said. "Steffi was worried about you. I looked all over, until I heard you crying in here."

"I remembered what David told me," I said. "The last time I saw him. I haven't been able to remember until now. It shook me to remember after all this time."

"That's understandable," he said. "Do you want to stay here?"

I dug some tissues out of my pocketbook and blew my nose. "No," I said. "I don't need to. I'd like to wash my face and go back to lunch."

Bill laughed. "Lunch ended five minutes ago," he said.

"We'll be late for history," I said, and got up, grabbing his hand as I did. "Come on."

"It's okay," he said. "Just don't wash your face. Those tears are alibi enough."

So we got up and walked to history together. And sure enough, there were no questions asked.

I'm still feeling pretty strange about it all. At peace for knowing that I couldn't possibly have known. But a little empty too. So much of my time's been devoted to trying to remember. And now I remember. And there's really nothing to tell.

December 23

Dr. Collins heard me out. I told him everything, from finishing the last of David's notebooks to remembering what he'd told me. He's the only person I've told everything to, and it felt odd to go over it all out loud, to share it all with someone.

"Don't expect the grief just to go away," he said. "Grief isn't like that."

"I know," I said, although I guess a part of me did think it would all vanish. "But I'm going to be okay. I know that now."

"Yes, you will be," he said. "You're going to be just fine, Lynn."

I smiled. It was like getting an A+ from my hardest teacher.

"You can be proud," he said. "It's been hard, and you've worked at it."

"Yeah," I said, still smiling. "I wonder . . ."

"What?" he asked.

"Just one of those what ifs," I said. "Remember the what ifs?"

"Of course," he said.

"I just wondered what I would have been like if David hadn't . . . if he hadn't killed Bob and Lorraine and himself. I guess that's too big a what if to speculate about."

"You would have been different," Dr. Collins said. "But not necessarily better."

"No," I said. "Not necessarily better."

December 27

Jimmy's been home for vacation for a couple of days now, and it's wonderful to see him. We caught up with each other's news, and we talked about David as well, but not nearly as much as we did over Thanksgiving. There were other things to talk about. We stayed up late again, comparing trivia and just enjoying ourselves.

I can't remember ever feeling so close to my family before.

January 1

For as long as I can remember, Mom and Dad spent New Year's Eve with Bob and Lorraine. David would spend the night here, and our parents would first have dinner out, then go to any one of a half dozen parties they were invited to.

Jimmy and I only spoke about it briefly, but we were both concerned about how they would cope with New Year's this time.

Mom and Dad made plans to spend the evening with the Gottliebs; they were having a small dinner party. Bill asked me to a party, but I decided to stay home. Parties still make me nervous, and New Year's Eve parties always try so hard. I didn't think I was up to the effort quite yet. Jimmy accepted an invitation though to a party friends of his were giving.

Mom and Dad both dressed up for the occasion, and they looked great. At eight they got into the car and drove off. I'd watched for signs of melancholy in them before they left, but honestly couldn't find any. So I settled in for an evening of watching football.

I was asleep when they got in and didn't have a chance to talk alone with Mom until just before noon. We sat in the kitchen, and she told me all about the Gottliebs' party, who'd been there and what they'd worn.

Finally, I couldn't stand it. "Didn't you miss Bob and Lorraine?" I asked. "Didn't you think about them?"

"Of course, we did," Mom said. "We associate New Year's with them, the same way you do. And we missed them this year. But they're dead now, and we're not. They wouldn't want us to mourn for them forever. As a matter of fact, we did exactly what they would have wanted us to. We went out last night and had a very good time."

She got up, walked over to me, and bent down to kiss my forehead. "In a way, that was the most fitting tribute we could give them," she said. "To them, and to the new year."

And I knew she was right. Not only that, but I was happy for her and Dad.

Happy New Year, world.

June 8

Today is David's birthday, a date he celebrated with the most remarkable ambivalence. I guess it's natural in someone who's adopted to feel funny about his birthday. Perhaps David's unusual reaction to it was perfectly normal.

Anyway, because of the date, David's been on my mind a lot more the past few days than he has been in a long time. Last night I dreamt about him for the first time in almost a month.

He knocked on the door, and I let him in. He looked good. He looked happy.

"I'm going away," he told me, as we stood in the front hallway.

"I know," I said.

"My parents are going with me," he said. "I'm taking them."

"I know that too," I said.

"Will you miss me?" he asked.

I nodded.

"Good," he said. "I don't want to be forgotten."

"I won't forget you," I said. "I promise."

"Think of me sometimes," he said. "Maybe not often, but every now and then. When you see a good photograph maybe, or hear a guitar. Is that too much to ask?"

"No," I said. "That's not too much. I'll think of you then."

"Good," he said. "Then I can be going."

"Take care," I said.

"I'll do what I can," he said. "Be happy, Lynn."

And when I watched him leave, I felt sad but at peace. I knew where David was going there would be no pain.

When I woke up, I cried a little, but not very much, and I fell back asleep fairly easily. And when I woke up this morning, and was filled with thoughts and memories of David, I knew it was because of his birthday, and not the dream. So I went downstairs and Mom mentioned first that it was David's birthday today. Dad asked if we remembered David's sixth birthday party, when he ran out sobbing because Annie had hit him and he hid in our bathroom for close to three hours, and would only unlock the door when he had everybody's sworn assurance that all the guests had left, but the presents they brought were still waiting for him. And we laughed at that and ate our toast, and I guess in our own different ways saluted his memory.

I got a letter last week from Jeffrey. I guess it belongs in this notebook, so I'm going to Scotch-tape it in right here.

June 1
Clear Brooks School

Dear Lynn,
Next week is David's birthday, and I guess be-

cause of that, and graduation, you've all been on my mind a lot. I singled you out to write this letter to, but please give my regards to everybody else.

Things here are pretty interesting. Between regular therapy sessions, group sessions, and academic stuff, I keep busy. There's a wide variety of kids here, all crazy naturally, but with a thousand different complaints. I've learned a lot here, about how easy it is to lose control, and how hard (but not impossible) it is to regain it.

I'll be graduating here later this month, and I've been provisionally accepted by Princeton (they get to change their mind if I have a psychotic episode between now and September). I think once I really started to learn, I learned a lot more here than I would have back home, since the classes are quite small, and none of us suffered from senioritis (the only disease we seem to be lacking).

It seems to me that I was pretty awful before I came here. I really don't remember too much after David died, but I have a vague recollection of giving you in particular a hard time, and I'd like to apologize. I was very mixed up then (obviously), and was having a rough time differentiating between reality (which was scary enough) and fantasy.

There's a boy here who tried to kill his father and mother. At least, he shot at them. He missed them, so he really isn't sure he meant to hit them, but talking with him has given me some idea of what David went through. We don't have many "criminal" types here though; mostly kids like me who hit a hard part in their lives and couldn't cope with it.

Anyway, once again, I'm really sorry if I gave you a bad time earlier. I'm not sure yet what my plans for the summer are, so I don't know if I'll see you before school starts in September. If I don't, have a pleasant summer and good luck in the years to come (how's that for a yearbook inscription?).

> Yours,
> Jeffrey

It's funny he mentioned the yearbook. I just got mine yesterday. I didn't work on it, so I was surprised at how often David popped up in it. No picture, of course, but the pictures of the junior class play are credited to him, and he's listed as official photographer. There are a couple of other pictures from sophomore and junior year that are his, and he shows up in one picture as well. He was something I think we'd all forgotten about, sophomore class treasurer (Bob and Lorraine pushed him into that one, of course).

There is one other picture of him in there. Tracy had gotten the idea last year to do a collage of pictures of some of us from first grade for an art project. It was decided to reproduce it as a front piece. So there we all are, Tracy, Judd, Annie, Charlie, Jeffrey, David, and me. How funny we all look. So earnest, with only a few of those patently false smiles. Staring out at what? Thinking what about our futures?

Right now I'm thinking very concretely about my future. Barnard put me on their waiting list (my grades did noticeably drop first semester this year), but U of Chicago accepted me, and I'll be going

there. I haven't given up on Barnard yet, and may
transfer there if I don't like Chicago. In the mean-
time, Mom and Dad think it's a good idea for me to
get away, and they had their doubts about New York
being the proper distance. They may well be right. In
any event, I'm looking forward to going there. Judd
will be there too, so I'll know at least one other kid,
which ought to help.

I have no particular plans for this summer, except
to work some at the gallery. Jimmy's planning to stay
in school and take some extra courses, so we won't be
seeing much of him (although I may go up there and
visit him for a change).

Tomorrow, by mutual consent, will be my last day
in therapy. Dr. Collins and I agree that I've gotten
what I needed from the therapy. I've made a successful adjustment to David's death.

I guess that means I can eat in the cafeteria now
just like everybody else and bike past the Morris
house and no longer get the shakes taking the train
into New York. I sleep better now, and no longer
carry a wad of tissues with me, just in case. I suppose
that constitutes successful adjustment.

Grief passes: change doesn't. I'm not the same person I was last September, and I'm not the same person I would have been if David hadn't done what he
did. Some of the changes in me are almost silly. I cry
at movies now and television shows (especially when
they're about the death of people my age) and even
occasionally at a book. I never did that before. I find
it very difficult to watch the news, especially the local
news coming from New York, which is always about
muggings and murders. I don't even like violence in
the movies (I had to leave one movie when people

started getting shot. It was that or throw up right there).

My feelings about people have changed as well. Steffi and I never really regained our former intimacy. We're friends again, thank goodness, but I almost never go over to her house, and she's rarely the first person I tell some things to. I'm more likely to tell Annie (using a walker now, and planning to graduate with the rest of us) or Bill.

If there's one change in me that I blame David for, it's the way things worked out with Bill. Granted there's a summer left, but I don't think anything's going to be very different between us. I like Bill an awful lot, and I know he likes me, but if David hadn't died, I'm sure we would have been a lot closer than we are. I could never totally break through my reserve with him. I don't know why, except that I'm more reserved with everybody than I used to be. I never really believed in unpleasant shocks before; now I have a hard time believing in pleasant surprises.

Sometimes I think about how many lives David changed that day. His, of course, and Bob and Lorraine's, but to a lesser extent, he affected an enormous amount of people. My whole family. Poor Jeffrey and his family and probably a lot of people there I don't know about. All the kids in school, including Bill, who never even met David. Mr. Glick, who is a lot less manipulative than he used to be (a change for the better; I guess change doesn't have to be negative). Dr. Collins. Lieutenant Donovan. Ms. Bullock who interviewed me at Barnard. A lot of people like that.

But there are more people as well. The reporters

for the papers, and the TV stations. The reporter for
Newsweek. All the people who read those articles or
saw the news items. Maybe even that poor boy in
White Plains who killed his family right after David
did. And all those people's families and friends.

And the changes won't stop this year. They may
never stop. Maybe twenty-five years from now one of
us will behave ever so slightly differently because
David could no longer endure his misery. I, for one,
know I'll be a different sort of parent than I might
otherwise have been. Or I might not be a parent at
all. More than most people, I know the risks.

Life really does continue though. The Squabblers
are finally making peace among themselves. The Morris house has been repainted, the windows repaired,
and real estate agents are showing prospective buyers
through it. Mom says she wouldn't be surprised if
someone moved in by September, in time for the new
school year. The lawn is mowed there now, and it
looks as well kept as it did when David lived there.
This was an unusually good year for Bob's tulips and
daffodils; his garden glowed with color.

David's notebooks are locked up in the safe; I had
Dad put them there as soon as I got them back from
Donovan, and I've felt no urge to take them out and
reread them. Still, I'm glad I didn't destroy them. I
think when I'm through with this entry, I'm going to
put this notebook in a sealed envelope, and give it to
Dad to put next to David's. After all, it's about David
really. It belongs there with his.

There are moments now when I have to think to
remember what David looked like, moments when I
have to concentrate to hear his voice. But what he
was, his love and his pain, have become a part of me.

I see things differently because of him. I feel things differently as well.

I wish David peace. That's really all I wish for any of us. Just simple peace.

ROBERT CORMIER
Unrelenting suspense.
Uncompromising endings.

☐ THE CHOCOLATE WAR

Jerry Renault, a New England high school student, is
stunned by his mother's recent death and appalled by the
way his father sleepwalks through life. At school he is
forced into a psychological showdown with his school's
secret society, the Vigils, for refusing to be bullied into sell-
ing chocolates for the annual fund raising $2.50 (94459-7)

☐ I AM THE CHEESE

Adam Farmer is a teenager on an arduous journey to find
his father. But what exactly is Adam looking for? Where is
his father? Why does Adam have two birth certificates?
Who is Paul Delmonte? What is the meaning of his parents' whispered conferences? Of their sudden move to a
new town, or the strange Mr. Grey who appears and
reappears in their lives? And why are Adam's thoughts
constantly interrupted by an unidentified interrogator
who prods him to recall some recent, devastating catastrophe? $2.50 (94060-5)

 LAUREL-LEAF BOOKS

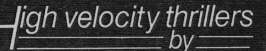